This signed, limited edition of

THESE LIFELESS THINGS

is one of only 300 copies and is

number

SATELLITES

THESE
LIFELESS
THINGS

First published 2021 by Solaris
an imprint of Rebellion Publishing Ltd,
Riverside House, Osney Mead,
Oxford, OX2 0ES, UK

www.solarisbooks.com

ISBN: 978 1 78108 990 3

Copyright © Premee Mohamed 2021

The right of the author to be identified as the author of this work has been asserted in accordance with the Copyright, Designs and Patents Act 1988.

All rights reserved. No part of this publication may be reproduced, stored in a retrieval system, or transmitted, in any form or by any means, electronic, mechanical, photocopying, recording or otherwise, without the prior permission of the copyright owners.

This is a work of fiction. All the characters and events portrayed in this book are fictional, and any resemblance to real people or incidents is purely coincidental.

10 9 8 7 6 5 4 3 2 1

A CIP catalogue record for this book is available from the British Library.

Designed & typeset by Rebellion Publishing

Printed in the UK

THESE LIFELESS THINGS

Premee Mohamed

For those who say:
Let us remake the chain.

April 28

Today we dug up bones in the Botanical Garden.

I was briefly, reflexively confused: How did these get here? But what a question. People just die wherever they die.

V. stopped digging too, and we studied our findings: brown, glistening, not white and dry like in the movies—for a moment I thought my eyes had tricked me, and we had found a layer of mulch. Or wood, a sculpture carved by some macabre but competent art student. Bone fragments fell on the trays at my feet, the strawberry runners we scavenged from the wall yesterday.

I just wanted something sweet. I haven't had anything sweet for a long time.

V. poked the skull with his boot and said: The grass in cemeteries, they say, stays green even in drought, because it drinks from the bodies of the dead.

I said, Who says that? That's disgusting.

He laughed, and I put my hand on his warm back in the black shirt—he's strong, there's still muscle along with the bone—and I thought, We could make love right here! In the sun! Right here under the gaze of God! Who, in this dead city, would stop us?

But, well.

We planted the strawberries, and more beans, and weeded the potatoes. In the fussy, preciously-laid-out Mediterranean gardens we scraped aside the white gravel, laying bare the black fabric below, in another SOS sign. Very satisfying, that noise.

No one's coming, I said.

Still, said V.

The soil rumbled and churned under our boots, not with the vigour of spring seedlings, nor worms or springtails or mice. Faceted, iridescent eyes watched us. A tiny tentacle lunged up and tugged impishly at my laces; V. spun at once and killed it with a blow from the spade.

I thought the soil at least had been spared, he said.

We'll see who spares who if they touch my strawberries, I said.

A good day's work. No sentinels seen. About half the remaining trees have turned, but watched us rather than attacking. We scrambled back to safety just before sundown, sweaty and thirsty as always, and joyously locked the doors and pulled the shutters behind us. Dark now. Something scrabbling on the street below.

* * *

"Emerson."

The botanical gardens. The botanical gardens. Quick, where is that on the map? Pull it up, check the drone photos...

"Emerson?"

I look up, dazed. "Wha?"

"We're just breaking for lunch, if you want to come."

I lower the book to my lap with trembling hands. I should be wearing gloves. No. Wait. The scanner can filter out my fingerprints. But that means I'll have to wait until I—

"Em!"

Winnie stoops and taps my wrist briskly with her sharp, painted fingernail. The pain is bright and minute as a wasp sting, and brings me back to myself, back to the cool gloom, the ceaseless breeze. The patch of sunlight I have been sitting in all morning has become shadow, violet and even scarlet around the edges from the dust in the air.

"Are you all right?"

"I found... I *think* I found," I correct myself professionally, "I think I *may have* found a... a primary source."

"Christ! Are you sure?"

"No. I don't know." I'm cradling the book, I realize, in both hands, close to my torso, as if I've picked up a small animal. "There's no date. The book itself was published fifty years pre-Setback. But it talks about the sentinels. About things in the dirt..."

Winnie watches me for a minute, her face politely interested but dubious. She's a forensic osteologist, or whatever her department is calling them now—the dropdown menu on the funding form didn't have our real titles, but we had to put something in to get the money—and she deals with trace chemicals, microscopic fragments, strands of hair, things that can be measured and tested. Journals don't fall under the purview of what she considers 'real science.' "Well, that's great," she says, her voice as sincere as she can make it. "We're meeting back at the pod," she says eventually. "In 14C. I'll keep yours hot."

"Thanks."

When she's gone, her microboard silent along the rubble-strewn street, I set the book down where I found it, and don the gloves in the back pocket of my cruise vest, and pick it up again. My heart is beating very fast.

The rest of the team might not help me. But I'm already thinking: *Beg Winnie to check the gardens for bone fragments. Ask Victor about the trees. What does 'turned' mean? It's too early in the year to be referring to fall.*

This could be my whole degree. My whole *life*.

May 1

I've taken to carrying this book in an inner pocket, tucking the pencil inside it so I don't lean over and puncture a lung (not that I can keep it that sharp, ha ha). What a funny thing to do, I keep thinking. I've made it a substitute for my phone. An object of both comfort and utility, like the plastic dollies that N. used to drag about when he was a little boy, the younger brother who never had a real baby to cuddle.

Now, I cradle the analogous-but-not-quite flat rectangle in my hands at spare moments, softly lit through dirty windows, and I imagine I could cry out, receive a reply within seconds, hear how people are doing. Loved ones. Friends. The world.

The world.

If this is to be the gradual petering out of what I thought of as the world, then so be it. But I am fiercely and adamantly and unshakeably and secretly sure that it is not.

I can't tell my theory to V., he'll laugh at me. But just as Hiroshima did not happen everywhere, just as the Shoah did not happen everywhere, just as the Great Hunger did not happen everywhere, I feel certain that there are places which were spared the Invasion.

Certain that... humanity, progress, evolution, whatever we were doing at the time (whatever that was, even though it may have been failing), <u>continues somewhere</u>, and that they who go on elsewhere have been prevented from helping us due to external circumstances of perhaps politics or finances or logistics or weaponry limitations. That they are not waiting for the sieges to lift and then to come count the dead, but that they are making preparations to rescue us.

Certain that one morning, we will awaken to find the rest of the world singing songs of gladness and coming over the horizon in huge, monster-proof helicopters...

...but They're not really monsters, are They?

They're something else.

At any rate, writing in here gives me something else to think about; and it lets me imagine that, once we're rescued, my words could join the words of others like me.

I don't want to say remnants. I don't want to say leftovers. I think I want to say 'survivors,' but... not if I don't survive.

Perhaps someone will read this and figure out what happened, because God knows I won't, and can't; I'm too busy.

We were trailed by sentinels today, who must have been watching us in the garden; their unevenly-scaled bodies were covered in white gravel from where they scrabbled in our sign. As night fell and we ran for cover, I wounded (I think) one statue, but did not kill it. One of the uglier ones, its twisted face scattered with spiraled teeth and eyes, shoulders humped with brass muscle. I would not have wanted to see that one begin to move.

Hang on. Something outside, not on cobblestones but wall. Something is breaking apart the plaster. Bastards! More later.

BY THE TIME I return to the research pod, the purple nanopolymer looming gaudy and self-conscious over the pale ruins, the others are almost done eating. Winnie hands me a bowl and gestures at the crumbling block of concrete next to Victor.

"Where's Fearless Leader?" I ask, tugging on the tiny foil strip of the heating nub.

"18A, I think," Victor says. "Near the river."

I'm almost too excited to eat, and I'm grateful for the two minutes my food takes to heat up. I feel like I'm a little kid again—or no, like the day my acceptance letter came. Sitting there with winter sun and icy air coming in through my window as sharp as a knife but not feeling it, instead something hot ballooning inside of me till it seemed to push into every corner of the room, reading it and re-reading it again and again. I am angry that my body needed to put the book down to eat.

I force myself to mechanically spoon up the too-salty, reconstituted pasta while my mind races. What I hoped to find here was never anything as good as this. A firsthand account of the Setback! Of course everything before is valuable, of course everything afterwards is valuable. Of course it is. But we have so many of those, and we have so very few of those three years themselves. Particularly in blockade cities. Off the top of my head, based on the literature review I did last semester, we have a grand total of *six* verifiable documents.

All four of us are studying different things, so it's not fair to compare what I've found with what they're going to find, but still. I could *dance*.

After lunch, when the others are gone, I feed my paper bowl into the digester, and then much more carefully feed the book into the scanner, after three diagnostic checks. Overkill, I guess. But this book is so precious, I simply can't risk it.

This isn't just my master's degree. This is my obsession, it's my life in a way; it's the only thing I've ever wanted to know about. Why some cities and not others is the small question. But the large question is: What happened?

Why does no one know? Why do even the people who lived through it not know? Why do my parents, my grandparents not know?

And then this, this miracle book. Maybe it will not answer any of these questions. Maybe it will peter out in a splatter of blood. I've had my heart broken before.

But the hope, the hope of it all, in this soft ancient paper, in the blockily tumbled edges of it, the smell of it. It's not even a proper journal, it's a poetry book, thick, one of those anthologies they give to first-year English students, with wide margins—probably why the writer picked it. I would have overlooked it if it hadn't been meant for us to find, displayed with a sign, a scrawled note on the wall: BOOK. So many books were burned for fuel in these cities when people couldn't get out to get wood or charcoal. The writing—smudged and tiny but impeccable—winds around and around each central poem in the wide margins. You can't help but think of something circling the drain. No. Less morbid. They lived, after all—lived long enough to write dozens of pages after the Invasion.

I thought it was encoded at first, but it's just that the lines crisscross and meander as they circle. It's not hidden. It was meant to be read. Maybe not by me. And of course, in my line of research, there's always that little nagging thought—would they *mind* if I read it? If I touched it, scanned it, reproduced it, published it? I often get the impression that they would hate it. It seems so disrespectful to the dead.

Maybe not in this case though; this writer, I feel certain, would be excited to know that we are studying it now.

That the 'world' of which they spoke started over again, picking up what pieces still remained, building something clumsy and slow and new, but (we hope) good.

I would tell them: I know. I know. It's been fifty years and we haven't yet figured out what happened. But we're doing our best to answer the questions. Make sense of it all, write a story out of history, which is not in and of itself a story—which tells us it is, because one event causes another, but it isn't. Not really. It's a series of scary fairytales to tell children in the dark.

Still shaking, I take out my own notebook, key to a fresh page, and begin to write.

May 3

A cool, clear day. Glad the everpresent clouds finally lifted; I see them on the horizon though, waiting to pounce. Do you think They affect the <u>weather</u> at all? I asked V.

He shrugged. It does seem different now, he said at last. But I can't quite put my finger on it.

Nightmares were bad last night. Faces swimming from the darkness, angular and harsh; staring eyes, membranes, flickering things like wings. The problem is that nothing They possess can actually be thought of as analogous to anything that anything on Earth possesses, if that makes any sense. Even mouths, eyes, all wrong. I heard Their songs chanting and wailing, and woke up screaming. Then I realized I had not dreamt the hollow, echoing booms of something striking the cement in the canal outside the flat. I know that sound.

This morning I found the expected: a dead man in the canal—a dead <u>stranger</u>, which should be impossible now, in this empty city. Still I studied his silvery, fallen-in face, hoping for recognition. He had drowned; I knew the bluish tone of the skin. A pearly sliver of eye white, no iris, showed under his upper lids.

He must have fallen into the canal running from Them and couldn't get back out. I suppose that's a better death than the one They would have given him. And yet in Their rage They'd still mauled the poor body. The statues and the sentinels sometimes move like the bigger ones, that herky-jerky movement—so swiftly it seems to be in the seconds between seconds, or so slowly they seem perfectly still.

I exhausted myself trying to haul him out. My back hurts now as I write. When V. came over we pulled him out together, then performed the necessary theatrics of death and stood around awkwardly for a while as if waiting for applause, or for someone to heckle us.

We should say a few words, I said after a while. I did not say: Because it may be our fault that the sentinels came upon him; why else would he be here? I thought: Let's give him a decent burial. Decent always means guilty.

How strange that I do not know his face, V. said, and then folded his hands and quoted some poem I did not know. The unexpected piety of the young! He fixed his gaze upon the bright empty sky, then lost all his sense, as often happens now, and nearly fell into the canal himself. I dragged him back at the last minute. I heard nothing.

I washed the dead man's jacket after dinner. Before all this, I never would have worn such a thing; but now,

now... I have so little, I carry everything I own on my back, I have made peace with it. The jacket will be temporary as we are all temporary. Like moving flats every couple of months and forgetting them at once. There is only now, there is no then. Must keep reminding myself of that. And keep this diary, to remember the now.

I must try to make entries every day instead of just when I'm too exhausted to do anything else.

Every day for years I've thought: I'll only get more tired, not less. And every day it turns out to be true. I thought I would have passed some kind of... event horizon of exhaustion by this point, but still the body digs up its reserves of strength from somewhere, as if it were a vein of metal buried so deep that no human art could ever find it, let alone extract it.

No mirror in this room. But I tried on the jacket a minute ago. Even damp, it is warm when it's zipped up, and hangs almost to the middle of my thighs. The punctures in it are cruciform, X-shaped; they beg the question: What made them? But there are so many potential answers.

Jacket hung back up to dry. I'll wear it tomorrow, when we go shopping.

May 5

Spent the day going door-to-door, industrious little bees, with our bucket and paintbrush, our axe and hockey stick. Just like those first days. People will become like animals, my husband said, and I agreed, and I wept with fear waiting for our door to be smashed in, for him to be killed and eaten in front of me, for myself to be raped in half while everything in my flat was stolen or broken. But it never happened; and if you knock, now, survivors invite you inside, and you put your axe in the umbrella stand. There are too few of us to fear the violence of the mob. There are too few of us, to be honest, to field a proper mob. We're more of a club.

Four big bags of questionable cans and canisters and packets, carted effortlessly back to the flat. I'll catalogue them tonight, start distributing them the day after tomorrow if I can. I need to rest. My breath rasps in my throat.

A funny thing. On Shoemaker Street we discovered— in fact, almost walked into—a new crater, house-sized, so fresh the soil was still damp and steaming below. Something misfired, I said, and V. nodded. I've never seen one so small.

In the house opposite, the only sign was a gleaming shard of metal embedded in the brick like a thorn. Perfectly clean, so smooth you could see your face in it. We walked over and did just that, and laughed and preened, far from the edge of the crater, listening to the soil shift.

Perhaps he was thinking of the day we met. It feels like another lifetime, though it was right after the invasion, before the city was really dead. Back when we still thought what government that remained might return things to normal.

Does he remember? The bomb hit as I was buying tomatoes from the marketplace, and sat hissing and spinning in the dirt. Another dud, I thought, but I still leapt to pull the tomato girl out of the way, knocking over the plastic tub; we both looked like we were covered in blood.

But it didn't go off, and I wandered away eventually from the football-sized thing and sat on a bench to eat. The trees had just begun to turn, and their tentacles craned to stare at me, the leaves wide-eyed, curious. I used to hate that, seeing <u>eyes</u> on the trees. Funny what you can get used to.

Then there he was, approaching me out of nowhere, a ragged skinny thing like a feral cat, slipping between the shadows of the watchful trunks. He was so very catlike back then, as if he might get a pat or a scrap by offering himself to a stranger, but still ready to run. He seems more settled now. I gave him a tomato, and the tiny paper packet of salt, and looked at him in the hazy sunlight, that Baltic olive skin and curly dark hair all cluttered with gold from the sun. The days, I thought, when we could rebuild. I did not know how wrong I was then.

But he's still here. And I'm still here.

Instead of fobbing him off as a thief or murderer I gave him my three-quarter profile, like a bullfighter, and held out my hand. In the distance at last, as we shook, a muffled explosion.

We were not imaginative enough, that was our problem, we pointed at the past and said, That cannot happen again, and we bought the science fiction books and said, That will never happen, and then everything happened and we were shocked, utterly unprepared, the news told us in the first five minutes ten million people killed themselves.

But they must have been fundamentalists, we said.

Evangelicals, radicals.

No: it was everyone, we simply did not imagine it.

After the world ended I thought we would resemble the dusty movies of the eighties, you know, studs, spikes, leather. Instead we all look like extras from Fiddler on the Roof, our clothes worn-down, exhaustively beaten up at the riverside, mangled and hung in the sun. M.'s old leather coat, bought aspirationally, non-ironically, long after those movies came out, protected me from the fires the night They came, and I had to throw it out. O noble cattle, that saved my skin!

I haven't seen a cow in over two years. But I know they are still out there, somewhere outside the wall. If I ever see one again, I will thank it.

Or, well. Let's be realistic. Eat it, and then thank it.

We thought the world would burn, disintegrate. Instead it simply flopped over and sighed, like a sick dog, and died in the street, and the buildings sagged instead of collapsing, and no one can drive cars now, and the gangs of feral cannibal children smugly sporting the wristwatches and sunglasses of the dead never materialized.

And yet. And yet.

Trapped and freezing, we did eat our dead that winter, swiftly, sensibly, as if in our genes, long inured to famine, some memory had resurfaced to tell us that history was happening again. I remember sitting next to V. when it really got bad, watching him quietly forking chunks of flesh off his plate in the shadow of those eroded, tottering skyscrapers, all pocked and ropy with mould, and the old woman at my side nudging me, telling me we must save our canned goods, eat the fresh stuff first. She is probably still alive somewhere in the city. The old women of our country are impossible to kill by normal means.

I told myself: I won't, I won't do it. Definitely not if it's... if it looks like... But it didn't, and I did. I thought it would taste like pork, but those first few bites tasted like freedom. A little bitter. Maybe we cooked it too rare.

Some of those old women were old enough to have survived the famine, I thought at the time.

I said to V., It's lurking there in the genes. Something for survival. Something that lets you do what's needed to outlast.

He said, patiently, Genetics doesn't work like that.

I said, It does too. I read an article about it. In Scientific American. There's something... they pass it on, they do. If your parents starve, their bodies remember, and then the genes of the children are ready, they are <u>already ready</u> for them to starve, from the moment they're conceived.

No, I don't believe so, he said, but he sounded uncertain.

That night, eating over the fire, I referred to Them as our conquerors, and Valentin hissed, Don't say that!

Eventually, we took back all the names that we came up with anyway. Now, everyone just says Them. And we all know. And though I have no way of knowing what the rest of the world is doing I am sure that in every language the people just say: Them.

V. still had war eye, back then. The bombs fell constantly, the population of the city halved overnight, then halved again, then again; we railed at whoever had mustered up a plane and some munitions trying to kill Them, who failed and were killing us instead, while the statues writhed and came alive, while They Themselves flickered in and out of existence from strange angles and passed through bodies like a killing mist, while the air was filled with dust and smoke.

Oh, that feverish burn! We all had it. They occupied our land, and then They occupied our eyes, after the skies split and the ground split and They roared up, half-seen, a blur, a glitch in the air, hints of eyeballs, tentacles, hair, scales, claws and teeth. So many of us had that look that we thought you could get some kind of disease from simply having seen Them. We didn't know it was just the shock and the exhaustion and the dust. The oldsters knew. Saw it before. Taught us to bathe our eyes in eggcups and build fires so the smoke rose up instead of out.

War eye. And I wouldn't even have known the term if not for those old ladies.

I KNOW I'M asking questions I'll never be able to answer, though I should research for a thousand years, visit a million of these cities. (I guess that's the point of academia, God help me.) But look at the questions my writer is asking now that we are here together. Their words and my words.

The Invasion. Witnessed, disbelieved at first, then a part of life. The writer is wrong, though—it *was* everywhere. Simultaneous and worldwide, as far as we can tell. The only difference was with cities like this, where some were barricaded to trap the residents there. And now I see the writer says 'siege' rather than blockade. That's rather good. In my notes I think I'll start calling it a siege city rather than blockade city. After all, that's what it was.

The war that created their siege began so easily: the movements of the Invaders reliably disrupted and then destroyed anything electromagnetic, so it would have been difficult, except on a very small, local scale, to tell what was happening; people would have had to sneak in and out of the city, and as the Setback continued, that would have grown progressively difficult.

Don't get attached, I tell myself, but...

No one was coming for you, my brave writer. I am so sorry. No one was coming, ever.

There: two years. That accurately dates it to the year. And one year before the end of the Setback.

The repeated mention of the statues. The others won't believe me. No one's got any proof that these... these new things, these statues that began springing up, ever did anything except remind the conquered peoples that they had indeed been conquered, just as had been happening throughout history. Vain, vain conquerors, everywhere you went. Their faces slapped onto generic bodies, welded onto generic horses.

The fact that they all had certain similarities, though not resembling anything Earthly, helped with that theory. After all, if you invade someplace, you want some consistency in your monuments. But there is indeed mention of it. Again and again. *The statues move. They come alive at night.*

Based on the drone photos, we chose a flat, intact square to drop our research pod, which turned out to be about fifty yards from one of those statues. A small one, slightly taller than me if you took it off its plinth. Ugly, blank-eyed, verdigrised the same colour as the leaves. I've taken a hundred photos of it since we arrived. Tell me your secrets, I demand of it. Tell me.

Of course, what I really mean is: Don't tell me. Don't move.

The writer and the companion note the weather. It occurs to me that they would have no way of knowing that the dropped nukes did in fact change the climate temporarily. Not the nuclear winter their ancestors feared but the Long Spring that halved the numbers of the surviving Setbackers, already so minimal from the pre-Setback days. When ninety-nine percent of the population is dead or missing, ninety-nine point five percent might tip a species into extinction.

The Five, my writer would not have known about those. No TV, no phones, no internet, no radio. Electricity seemed to run (from our best estimates) anywhere from fifteen minutes to twenty-eight hours after the Invasion, but the Five didn't begin to fall until after that. They definitely had no idea that Taurus Gray fell practically in their backyard. I've seen no mention so far of fallout, radiation sickness, anything like that. They just wonder, idly, about the local weather.

And it turned out you couldn't nuke Them anyway.

That polite, academic fight with Darian back at campus, in Dr. Aaron's office. "Well where *did* They come from? Why can't I say extradimensional? They didn't come from space. We would have seen it. They weren't from Earth. Everything had been mapped at that point. They came from somewhere else, and They'd been here before, and They resented that They ever had to leave. That's our best theory, goddammit."

"When you say it like that, you make it sound like *magic*. Maybe you should quit reading fantasy novels for five minutes!"

He doesn't hate me. I don't think it's that. He doesn't even, I think, hate girls in general. But he didn't want me to come on this research trip, and even after I told him I'd applied I think he thought I'd never get funding.

The others are his kind of scientist. Numbers, tables. Winnie with her bone shards, and Victor the dedicated biologist. People who would publish papers that he'd actually read. Darian's never made it a secret that he thinks the only good that could ever come out of my research is publishing a ton of pop-sci books written in 'layman's language,' which he hates so much, and the only good would be me funding my own research and not tagging along with the 'real' scientists. He won't say it to my face. But I've heard enough.

Still. There's more than one way of knowing. I'll never convince them of it, but it's true.

May 18

I don't know why but it struck me as funny that V. came over this morning with a lead pipe. Maybe I haven't been sleeping enough, but I had to sit down on the steps and laugh. He stood there indignant, leaning on it.

Where did you get that, I finally wheezed.

Oh, come on, he said. There are exposed pipes everywhere, Eva.

I think I hurt his pride. Just when you think a man is different, it turns out he's just like all the rest. But I told him I had a stitch and he helped me off the steps, and even found me a pipe of my own, plain iron. Such chivalry!

Still, we argued as we walked, swinging our pipes. He wanted to go to the modern art gallery, I to the war museum or maybe the space memorial. We could do both, I said. There should be enough daylight.

Why bother? he cried. We need to preserve what is beautiful and good, not what only looks backward towards a past that we will never have again.

What, war? I shouted. You can't be serious. The past? It isn't even past yet. What do you think this is?

When this is all over, they won't call this a war, he said. A war implies that we fought back.

What makes you think anyone will be alive to call it anything? Anyway, I don't care, I said. And the crap in the modern art gallery can wait another day. You know They won't target it. There isn't enough metal in there, it's all... carbon-fibre and crap (I confess I may have said 'carbohydrate fibre' in my frustration).

I wanted him to understand that this place, our little city, has been destroyed again and again, despite being so small, so unimportant, nothing essential about us except that in the old days we were in the corridor between one big city and another, and then later that we had both the railway and the lake. In WWII they bombed us into a smear in the ground, and we rebuilt and rebuilt for years. Look at the state of our walls! We owe it to those people to protect the memory of their work. To throw it away is a slap in the face.

On we went, bickering, in the cold, light spring rain. Grateful it wasn't heavier (I hate how you can't hear anything approaching in heavy rain). In the muddy streets, fresh footprints, square or round or cloven, or disquieting traces of centipede, pillbug, octopus, snake. Slippery as hell. I regret not noticing that till later.

We darted into the museum, ignoring the smashed facade, using a side door. The glass splintered quietly under my pipe. I thought it was safety glass, I said. What if a child had run into that?

Why would someone be so cruel as to take their child here? he sneered.

Inside, we barricaded the broken door with chairs and desks, and trotted back and forth on the squeaky parquet floor, binding the statues with canvas and rope, padding exhibits with cotton baling and crumpled paper, till everything was unrecognizable. We took paintings and even tapestries off the wall and boxed them in the basement; out of habit, as the door swung open on the darkness, V. flicked the light switch. We both laughed. The desire for electricity does not die quickly or easily. I suppose in ten years, if either of us are still alive, we'll still be scrabbling for a light switch in dark places. We sandbagged a few of the huge monuments that were too heavy to move.

The museum staff made all these sandbags, V. panted. How did they ever find time?

Who knows, I said.

And why? Why not just leave, run?

I don't know, I said. You can't abandon <u>everything</u>.

Outside the barricades, things paced and snarled, suspicious; you could hear the noise over the rain. I've always wondered: can they smell? I know they can see; if you freeze, sometimes they'll lose interest and move on. But what other senses have they got? What do you get, if you're made of brass and magic, or the grab-bag of assorted junk that even the abyssal creatures cannot use?

And why do we bother, anyway, I sometimes think; but V.'s enthusiasm drags me along behind it, as if I am a young girl walking a very big dog, instead of a fortyish woman who might be (oh, for God's sake, just say it) falling in love with a twenty-five year-old, a bloody fool of a puppy with curly hair.

There was no time to discuss it as we left. Daylight, at least. But we stepped outside and I nearly swallowed my tongue: surrounded by sentinels, appearing silently in the rain.

Get them away from the museum! V. said, and I said WHAT?

Anyway. We ran, slipping in the mud, harried at our very heels. Some of the things can't move very well, and when they phase in and out of existence they end up wedged in walls and curbs. I panted in the cold rain, choked on it, coughed. They were watching us, of course. Listening to the things going on in there. But you never know whether they'll attack or just wander off. Bloody things.

We climbed to a rooftop at last, and with high ground were able to stun and perhaps kill (not sure) the two things that made it up there, and then it took forever to catch our breath. Even in the old days I couldn't have run like that.

You've got a death wish, I said to him.

No, he said. I just wanted to... I mean, after all the work we did.

You do, you do too. And so do I. What will become of us?

I thought he was going to argue, but he stopped, and put a hand on my shoulder, on my new coat, and he said, I've got a life wish. I want to live. And from now on, I'm not going to do anything but save my own life.

Then I've got one too, I said. And I'll make the same oath.

Good, he said.

His burning eyes under the wet lashes. Was he crying? Handy to have it happen in the rain.

When we got back to the flat he said, Were you a teacher or something? A professor at the university?

I didn't want to talk about it, but I couldn't think of anything to say, either. I stared steadily past his shoulder, at the window, and did not answer.

At any rate, it seems that we are both cursed to live.

June 2

Do you remember, V. said, as we chopped wood, and stopped and gasped, and chopped, and gasped again, the revolution?

I'm not that old, you little shit, I said.

Not that one. Or the other one. I mean the one after... after They came. Did you see?

Oh, yes, I said, straightening, putting a hand in my back. Chopping wood: so horrible.

Hands still blistered, hurts to write. I'll switch hands.

He waited for me to keep talking, but I shrugged: Yes, I remember.

I didn't see all of it; it was over so quickly, and it mostly happened downtown, where I often avoided going, since you couldn't run in the rubble.

It was a few months after the invasion, a few months before the city army assembled itself, that odd, twilight time, a soft and falsely liminal hour in which we were equally certain either that we would survive and rebuild, and that humankind was extinct and we just didn't know it yet. And just in that twilight, a group of people, young people, as so often happens, marched downtown, and armed themselves, and because you never know where They are, because bodies (They seem to think) are things that happen to other, lesser beings, the rebels merely built a mountain of shards and stones, and climbed it, and yelled, and waved flags, and announced their demands.

I can't believe it happened, I said.

What do you mean? said V.

I mean, how utterly stupid and naïve must you be to make <u>demands</u> of something that doesn't give a shit whether you live or die... I don't know, Valentin, what do revolutionaries do? They had no leverage, none at all. How else did they think that was going to end?

He jutted his jaw out; I had hurt him. I wondered, fleetingly, whether he, little draft-dodger, had been part of that group, the survivors who had fled and so lived; it must be hard to be a handsome revolutionary, I thought, you know, you're always wondering what version of you they'll use for the stamp, what for the statue; will they sculpt you when you are old and fat and you take a bullet meant for someone else in some little skirmish? Was he out there waving a flag, scared of being martyred? I wouldn't have been.

We didn't know about Them then, he said. We didn't know what They were, what They wanted.

We still don't know that.

What _do_ They want, do you think? he said. I've thought about it. Why us, why here, why now? Why Earth?

Maybe They'll tell us one day, I said. He seemed satisfied with that, and we got a good, big pile of wood to take back. Wonderful dry stuff from normal trees, thank God. Of course it'll need to season.

But I don't think They ever will tell us. I get the sense... sometimes, in my dreams, nothing I'd ever tell him... that They're so old that we're not even like insects to Them, which are a long and noble lineage to us, much longer than our own, silly apes as we are. We're barely noticeable. We're so far below Their notice that we're more like... bacteria or something, I don't know. Germs growing more or less invisibly in their canned jam, in the house into which they've moved with its nicely-stocked pantry, and they will only take action against a can if it starts to bulge or froth.

This is a terrible analogy. M. would have laughed at me.

Can you tell I'm craving sugar? So badly. I'm on the verge of sneaking out of the city to go eat a raw sugar beet. I even wish sometimes for a stray beehive, or colony I mean, I would risk the stings for a few bites of honeycomb, like a chimpanzee. But I haven't seen bees for a long time. I wonder if they pose too much of a threat to Them. You kill your enemies at once when they are most like you, of course. History shows us that.

A hive, a hive mind. I wonder.

Chocolate. Jam. Cream pastry. Nougat. Baklava.

Maybe we will find a jar of honey somewhere in this godforsaken city that someone hasn't looted.

Now just a minute though: <u>Have</u> we been forsaken by the gods?

Maybe They're the ones who showed up, calling 'New gods for old!' like in the fairytales. Well then, I wish They'd forsake us. Or tell us what They <u>want</u>. But at the same time, maybe we don't want to know. Maybe that's not something for our minds, the minds of the undivine.

Absolute compliance still results in death. It's not obedience They want. It's not (I think) food. They kill you, maul your corpse, but They don't eat you. Half the time They lose interest halfway through and flicker out of existence, leering with Their tangled teeth. Genocide is <u>happening</u>; is that Their goal? Or is it something else?

And where <u>is</u> everybody?

EVA, HER NAME is Eva. I'm weirdly struck by this, and how long it took me to get to it. Of course you don't use your own name when you write to yourself. I suppose I'm lucky to learn it at all.

It's chilly in the morning, but no one wants to eat inside the pod, adding the smell of food to the smells of feet and sweat and ink and electronics. We wrap up and eat outside, ready to set aside our scarves and gloves in an hour or so when it warms up, when the sun glints off the golden domes and focuses on us like a parabolic mirror. No one can identify what the breakfast pack is. Certainly, there are potatoes.

"Is this one of those... military meals?" Victor says cautiously.

"I think so," Winnie says. "It was a condition on the funding. Darian ordered it. We had to carry the highest calorie to weight ratio for the least cost."

"That should be impossible."

"Well, that's why we're eating this stuff."

"Two days down, ten to go."

"I'd rather eat the canned stuff at this point."

"Winnie, that stuff is fifty years old."

"Well, it's in a can, isn't it? If the seals held—"

I tune out their bickering, and clean off my spoon. We're all doing so much digging and walking and climbing, everywhere the boards can't go, and we're already hungry all the time, even in our sleep. I can't imagine having to survive in this city, constantly harried and hunted, alone and terrified. And waiting for a rescue that would never come...

"The SOS sign at the botanical gardens," I tell them, trying to stir up interest again. "I found a journal written by the people who made it."

"No shit?" Victor says, interested at last. "Hey, look at that. Primary source corroboration. I don't suppose they saved any seeds in that journal, did they?"

"Victor."

"Sorry, sorry. I live in hope."

The drone paths showed us intact statues, evidence of bombing, signal fires, SOS signs—many on rooftops, and one, just one, in what had once been pretty white gravel, surrounded by warm-temperature plants.

We picked this city because it's a good research city. And I may have found the most important document in the entire thing. But who cares, right? There's Darian out there, getting photomicroscopy images of the busted buildings to see if they were bombed, looted, attacked by Them; there's Victor, carefully dissecting seedlings and mice; there's Winnie with her portable lab, her little stable of human remains detection sniffer rats and crawlerbots. And me. Who reads diaries.

Sometimes I look around, wearily, and ask myself: Why aren't more people studying the Setback? Why isn't *everyone* studying it, why did we bother starting universities again, why did we rebuild them if not to figure out what happened? It knocked the entire world back to the stone age and everything had to be recreated from scratch. It was the greatest extinction event of a single species (us) in the history of the Earth, more than the K-T Event. We are the descendants of that zero-point-five percent of people who made it through those three years. Yet I *personally* know more people studying the Hundred Years War. Half of my friends are Renaissance scholars. Instead of the microscope of the world being trained on the Setback, everyone looked away.

I look at our research team and I wonder what the writer would have thought of us. Darian is the oldest, at twenty-seven, but all of us were born years and years after everything was over. We can't know what it was like. We can read about it, we can dream about it, but we can't *know*. This book is the closest I'll ever come to knowing.

I sit in the remnants of the botanical garden and go through the scans of the first entries, under what's left of the dome. They built it well; the iron bones jut bravely in their precise, original formations, exposed without their flesh of glass. The air is warm and damp, smelling of the sunflower fields outside the town. Before now, if you had told me that sunflowers had a smell, I wouldn't have believed you.

About the statues… I mean, no one seriously believes the statues were 'coming alive,' but neither are the specifics quite clear either. There is minimal literature coming from the survivors even now, they don't seem to want to talk about it and cannot be begged, coaxed, bribed, cajoled, nagged, bullied, or threatened into it (believe me), but they are *adamant* about the statues. And they all say, in their various languages, leaning forward into various microphones, meeting my eyes: Coming alive. But we don't know how.

And there is a significant struggle to identify the enemy, period, who left nothing but these statues, which *we* made, and their traces, like tracks in mud, that we have to analyze as if they were fossils. There is the unspoken assumption that since no recordings survived on the tech of the time, at least some of the facts were made up or exaggerated. Well. Unspoken for most of us. Darian says it all the time. That's why he's more comfortable with his X-rays, his instruments, his lasers, his busted buildings and crater measurements, his numbers.

I helped him last summer, against his will (Dr. Aaron, unaware, lent me out to his supervisor's lab), with a database on the purported earthquakes, tsunamis, volcanic eruptions, rifts, sinkholes, and so on, that supposedly happened during the Setback. "Look at this stuff," he sneered. "Like some ancient book whimpering about the Great Flood. That's how credible half this stuff is. Telling stories around a campfire, screwing it up with each re-telling."

"You'd have a lifetime worth of work proving it though," I said, strained, trying to be polite. "At least the evidence is recent. Not thousands of years old."

"I suppose so," he said grudgingly. "And at least for most of them there should be evidence."

"But there's—" I began, and stopped; we both knew I was going to say 'first-person accounts,' which he mistrusts and, I now think, with the experience of that summer behind me, hates.

Now, he walks past me and says, reminding me, "You're obsessed with that thing. Find anything else useful?"

Heavy in his smug voice is the reminder that plays in my head all day and even at night, in my dreams: We only have ten more days here. Make it count. And don't waste other people's time.

But I have to; I force myself to ask the others to help me recon the buildings, looking for clues from the journal.

"This will be the only time," I say, and try to keep the wheedling out of my voice. "Please. It'll only take a few hours, and maybe we'll find... we'll... find things for your projects too."

"All right," Victor says. "I walk around all the time anyway."

Darian looks at me stonily; his eyes are almost the same colour as the concrete, in his darkly tanned face.

"So you're looking for... what, exactly? Based on this diary?"

"Signs of marks on the doorways or walls. Showing which houses they looted. They said they had a bucket and a paintbrush. And, and, and"—I remember, and stumble over my words in my eagerness—"a bomb crater that was fresh at the time, two years post-Invasion. On Shoemaker Street. With a piece of shrapnel in it."

"They were still being bombed two years later?" he says, interested at last. "That's what they said? A fresh crater?"

"Yes! Brand new. The casing not even rusted, they said."

"Oh, all right."

All afternoon we scramble up and down the broken streets, tripping on cobbles, riding where we can, carrying the boards on our backpacks where we cannot. And we find nothing on any doorways or walls. "What colour paint did they use? Gray?" Darian grouses. I keep silent; there's no way to jolly him when he's in a mood like that, and you're better off not even trying.

We pause briefly at what is obviously the shrapnel, still, after all these years, embedded in the house, and he says, "There's no crater." I don't defend the journal, but nod; I should be yelling "Told you so!" because I am half-right even if it looks like I am half-wrong too, but I hang my head instead. Still, he point-marks the site and puts it in his notepad, and we keep walking, and he doesn't leave us.

Victor is less vocally disappointed and I find myself hanging back so we can talk; outside of my first-year biology class I don't really understand most of what he's talking about. Every now and then a familiar word bobs up like an iceberg in the ocean of his excited monologue.

I cut him off, tugging on his jacket. "This idea that Eva had," I said. "About there being a cannibalism... like a gene for it..."

"That's not the case," he says primly, but his face lights up. "All the same, you should ask Winnie about whether she's found any evidence of cannibalism in the bone fragments she's finding."

"I'll do that, thanks."

In fact I do it on my phone while he's still talking, waving his hands around at the lacy wrecks of the buildings around us, his bright yellow gloves the only colour for blocks around. No response from Winnie. I refresh the screen a few times, and shrug.

"Epigenetics," says Victor. "The research is just starting back up again. You know how it is. We had all the written research in the world, but all the experimental lines and organisms were long, long dead."

"Yeah. But it's not really—"

"No, no. What I meant to say was there's no cannibalism *gene* in humans. We've never found any evidence of that. But if you're thinking that a good number of epigenetic traits related to survival in general were activated in descendants, then yes, that's very likely. Metabolic management, things related to homeostasis in general. Body temperature management. Calcium cycling. Adipose storage. There's even evidence that the microbiome is different. There's likely to be phenotypic plasticity that's—"

"What?"

"Ah! You see it in some species. Let's say frogs. When tadpoles get overcrowded and food is scarce, some of them get a developmental leg up by eating their conspecifics. These ones, they get stronger jaws, sharp little nubs that look like teeth. The victims, I mean the food, the *prey*, don't. Visually, if you pick up a handful and sort through them, you can easily see which ones are cannibals and which ones aren't. That's how much they change. Their DNA doesn't change. But they all carry the genes needed to turn."

"Horror movie," Darian says, without turning around.

Victor jumps, nearly walks into a fire hydrant, and lowers his voice. "It's... it's a well-studied adaptation response to difficult environmental conditions. Traits that help digest meat and bone, too. Their digestive systems can't really handle it before the changes."

Idly, I think of the old ladies the writer refers to, and whether we would see, in their skulls, evidence that they were doing what they were supposedly doing. The teeth and jaws of monsters. But I don't think that happens in humans.

"These are our ancestors," I say slowly. "We inherited all that."

"Yes."

"And if there were... these epigenetic changes..."

"Well, certainly I would think so," Victor says. I find myself curiously interested in his teeth, white and uneven, and Darian's, large and sharp. He didn't even let me finish my sentence, but I suppose he knew what I meant.

But I'm bothered by it, and I corner Victor after dinner, in the starry dark, as we quietly work at our separate stations before bed. I apologize profusely for interrupting him, but he's running some kind of comparative DNA analysis on tree trunks and the fresh seedlings we've seen, and his computer is clearly busy, a progress bar taking up an inconvenient amount of the screen. He swivels on his sproingy chair and regards me brightly in the light of the LED lanterns. "Emerson! Pull up a... a concrete block."

"The writer thinks mostly old women survived," I say quietly. "But that's not how it would be in nature. Is it?"

"Oh, no. No, often not. Where the old survive, of course, it's because they're exhibiting traits that we would call human-like: culture, memory, problem-solving, even sociopathy. In general if there's that kind of... of... of *winnowing* in a survival situation, you'll find the young and strong surviving."

"Smaller chicks being pushed out of the nest if the parents don't feed both chicks properly. That kind of thing."

"Or the smaller chick being killed and eaten by the larger. It's just calories, you know."

"Victor."

"I mean, in nature," he says hurriedly.

"But people don't do that," I say. "Even in survival situations. We've found no evidence of... of that kind of thing during the Setback. Even in old material from concentration camps. People protect and shelter the weak, they don't kill them to survive."

"No? Airplane crash survivor demographics."

"What?"

He holds up a hand, and tilts it unhelpfully in the air. "When you look at the numbers of people who die in airplane crashes, people always want to think that it's whether you're in the nose or the tail or over the wings. Or whether you had just eaten, or were wearing your seatbelt, or... things like that. But when you run the real statistics on who makes it out alive, if anyone does, you'll find that for some reason it's males, aged 15-60, sitting anywhere on the plane. Way over the rates of women of any age, children of any age. What does that tell you?"

"I... I don't know. Maybe the weight, the distribution of muscle mass..."

"Nope. Try again."

But try as I might I cannot make myself say that it's clear, as Victor thinks it is, it's clear that that's because men are shoving people aside to get to the exits. None of this 'Women and children first!' like in the old movies.

Victor is a year younger than me, he's thin and looks flimsy, but he's a foot taller than me and I find myself wondering whether he'd push me aside if our plane was crashing. If he'd want to survive so badly that he'd do that. He smiles uncertainly at me, perhaps seeing my thoughts written on my face.

"You should sleep," he says.

"I've still got work to do."

"Oh?" He tries to take back his surprise, but it's too late. I'm not offended, really. I know what they think about my research, even if he's more polite about it than the others.

"Goodnight, Victor," I tell him, and stalk back to my station, and put up the paneling, and cry a little bit before I keep reading. Because of the colour schemes of their preferred software, the others glow all different colours in the darkness—Winnie is a soft violet, Darian's a gray-blue, Victor is pink and red. Mine would be gold, from the greeny-gold colour of the text reader, diligently transcribing my anonymous author's crabbed scrawl into a tight and readable text. I bet it would look pretty from above. Maybe tomorrow night I'll try to get a photo.

June 24

Horror yesterday. When we think we have seen more than our fill.

And shock, when we think we can no longer be shocked.

Just at dusk, a statue darted across the street in front of us, startling, like a stray cat—though of course much bigger, as big as a horse, but still the likeness was unmistakeable. And catlike it hesitated when it saw us, one paw up, spiked and clubbed like the bloated claw of a scorpion. The grotesque face remained in profile. And then we saw something in its muzzle, ragged and red. Another corpse, I thought wearily, but it writhed just as I thought this, and screamed, and I involuntarily lunged for it.

V. got a handful of my jacket and yanked me back. There are more, he whispered, and I barely heard him; in fact I did not realize what he said till later.

But we both saw it. The thing, the monster, had a <u>child</u> in its mouth. Not dead. Alive.

I pore obssessively over my memory of it, as if I am scrolling back and forth and zooming in on a photo on my phone, getting as close as I can till I can see nothing else. I'm shaking, my fingers are shaking.

A red coat, dark pants, dark boots, bright blond hair. The hair killed me. Stopped my heart. Just like both I. and N. when they were little, before it began to turn mousy... bright, bright blond, like the hair of a doll.

And the statue sprang away with a creak, the scream of its victim fading. A photo come to life.

Somehow I found myself with V. in the arch of a doorway, breathing hard, unspeaking. At my ear, the Byzantine grid of scribbled letters and names on the buzzer pad, my head striking it again and again in my eagerness to bolt. Let go, I said, and tried to wrench my coat free, and he said, You'll do something stupid.

Yes. Yes. I will. Let me go.

We waited far too long, perhaps half an hour, before moving again; the sun sank into full dark. I stared vacantly out at the long violet shadows moving across the buildings. We were in the oldest part of town, the medieval streets higgledy-piggledy, and if I had run after the thing, I would have fallen right off that stone drop and about ten meters into someone's backyard.

Have you seen Them eat people, I finally said, in what I was surprised to hear was a very normal tone of voice.

V. thought. I don't know, he finally said. I've seen the sentinels and the statues kill people with their mouths. But not eat the bodies. And I've never gotten a good look at Them. He paused. Then: Do you think They came here to Earth because people are food?

I don't know, I said. But if they aren't eating people, what was that thing doing with that little boy?

All the possible answers were too horrible to contemplate... and I really mean that, in this city where I have eaten, myself, human flesh, like a dog, like a fox creeping into the home of someone who has died, where I have killed my fellow man, been forced to kill, where I have seen the blood of my husband, where my children are gone from me, I can <u>barely contemplate</u> what the monsters are doing if they are taking children alive.

There was an evacuation, I said.

Yes, I remember that, V. said. Trying to get families out. About three months after the Invasion. And everyone died.

Well, they couldn't have known that would happen, I said.

But you didn't leave, he said. <u>You</u> thought it might happen.

Yes.

He paused: What should we do?

We have to tell the others, I said. Someone will know something.

He nodded. We're having another neighbourhood dinner this week. A. is hosting. I don't know why I have this faith that someone will know, but...

I'm so angry that They have taken fellowship from us. We eat in secret fortifications because They inevitably find groups and leap in like a wolf in the fold, as if there is nothing They hate more than that we might find comfort and safety with one another. We tire of the same faces again and again, and then any strange face means we panic, not knowing who works for Them. If only there were ways to tell. If only we were a little less tired, a little more awake.

That boy, that fading cry!

THE DESCRIPTION OF the Invasion is the same everywhere. As ridiculous as it sounds to us, we cannot write it off as mythology; it's history. And how strange, that Eva has noticed the usage of 'Them.' In every country, in every language, that's what people defaulted to. Now, with the distance that allows us to be merely uneasy instead of terrified, we call them 'the Invaders.' But back then you'd be too scared to think. You'd just say 'Them' and everyone would know what you meant.

I check the museums and galleries, and find the sandbagged statues that Eva and V. protected, the stashed paintings, and I race back to get the others. Panting, exhausted, we unbury them and stare. Light falls like chalkdust from the broken roof. Solemnly, one of the crawlers begins to climb the massed heap of sandbags, its claws digging into the rotten canvas, the only sound in the building. Dust filters down from the opened windows. Winnie nudges the robot down with her foot.

"Oh my God," she whispers. "You'll be famous!"

"We'll all be famous," I correct her, also in a whisper.

Darian snorts, and erases us with the flat of his hand, and goes outside, into the cleaner air. I'm not surprised. But something else bothers me, as we point-mark it and head back. It's that any of these things should still be intact after the events described in the journal. No one's touched them in fifty years. No survivors came in here seeking shelter or culture or scavenging for weapons or supplies. Half a century, and no one came back here? No one?

I don't like it. I mean, it's useful for my research (hell, that could be my PhD when I'm done my masters—something something study of returning residents in siege cities, if any) but it goes against everything I know about the post-Setback years from the things I've read. People craved fellowship, company, comfort. They coalesced again in their tiny bands of survivors, and they found cities to reoccupy. No one could build anything again those first years; you had to find somewhere with a solar farm or wind farm or hydro plant or something—something where you didn't have to drag in feedstock on trains or cars that no longer operated—so you could get electricity again. And that meant cities. And for some reason, it never meant the siege cities. Why? Once They were gone, They were gone. It would have been perfectly safe.

I don't get it.

But that's why we're here, right? To study. To guess. Even if we can't know.

My ears are starting to hum. I'm guessing that's from the enormous level of sodium in our food, and dehydration, and forcing my noodle-like legs to climb several flights of stairs an hour. Very strange though. And only at night.

* * *

June 25

Under the pretext of looking for dinner party food we returned to old town, swarming now with sentinels. Our waved pipes and thrown stones did not deter them (I'm a terrible shot anyway), and we fled, ignobly, our empty sacks whispering on our backs, like thwarted gnomes.

We moved uphill, twenty blocks away, and went through the rich houses that had of course been looted first—broken glass everywhere, and the kitchens empty, not even curtains blowing in the wind. I ran my hands over silk gowns, thick wool jackets. You can't carry all that, V. said from the other room.

You can't even see what I'm doing, I said.

I can hear you.

I fled any room with hints of toys or cribs, anything with little clothes or board books, I couldn't bear it, it was like entering a room full of poison gas. I could barely look for a second before my eyes began to tear up.

Everywhere we saw the signs of people succumbing to whatever They did to the brain in those first few days—empty nooses, guns, brain splatter, pill bottles. No bodies, for some reason. But the intricate sigils on the wall, drawn in ink or paint or blood, and the pitiful cries for help in ten languages.

Do you think they all really died? I said.

V. said, Or lost their minds and tried to join Them.

How do you join something like that? I said. That's like an ant trying to join a multinational corporation. Though I suppose that's what the agents are doing. If they exist.

I know, he said. But that happens in wars. Doesn't

it? People don't just... knuckle under the conqueror and nurse their grievances. Not everybody. They fire themselves up, put on their nice suits, sign up for the party or whatever. Not just play along. If they're genuine, they get, you know. Special favours. They survive.

Yes, I said, for betraying and killing their own people. I know our history too, you know.

I know, he said, dejectedly. It's human nature to betray.

They're up to something, I said.

They're not up to anything more than a nest of wasps is up to anything, V. said. They don't have <u>intent</u>. People just went crazy, that's all. From the pull, and the noise, and that damn singing, and the nightmares.

You don't know that, I said.

He shrugged; he was wrapping knives in a pillowcase and putting them in his sack. He said, They came here so suddenly. Maybe They'll just leave as suddenly. Maybe Their intent was to... gather resources or something, like in the alien movies, and They'll just leave.

As we pondered this incredibly trite statement I thought idly of how interesting it is that you can hear the capitalization in the name. Well, They are gods, are They not? You get the capital letter whether you earn it or not, if you are a god.

I want to know: How do we know They are gods?

But that is a limitation both of the divine and of our language when speaking of the divine. And no one said all the gods were <u>good</u>.

Anyway.

With our findings, I think I can feed the (appx.) eleven people left in our immediate neighbourhood; if A. is still hosting he'll get the word out first thing in the morning.

It's good, it's like a tiny census, and it's harder to betray people when you know their face.

I have a tuna, bean, and olive salad (like a Niçoise?) planned, with flatbread (oh, how I wish we had pasta; but I haven't seen a single egg in two years), and a kind of tomato sardine soup, with pickle garnish. I even found a little tin of caviar; everyone can have a spoonful. There will also be braised cabbage, we need the vitamins, but that's not really a <u>treat</u>. Maybe if we had some salo.

In those first starving days, when we couldn't get out to scavenge ('shop,' V. insists), I dreamed about meals far less elaborate than this; this would have seemed an impossible, fairytale feast. I thought about simple bread-and-butter, and plum jam from Baba's ruthlessly temperature-controlled pantry, boiled new potatoes, varenyky, all the things we ate when the boys were little and we didn't have much time to cook.

And then, after a while, I stopped thinking about food at all, preferring sleep; I could never get my fill, I wanted to sleep forever, but between the screams and the Them and the trees and the bombs, I would go—what was it, that first time?—maybe two weeks without sleep longer than an hour or so, day or night. God! Remember that. Don't forget that.

Now, because everyone is dead, and the Army is gone, there is both food and sleep. But there is no escape. We may as well have our fairytale feast.

If They are taking children alive, what are They feeding them?

Stop, stop. Someone will know. Someone will have heard something.

June 27

Mmm. The long, slow breath of the few dinner guests that did not get out by sunset, and opted to spend the night. They lie like dogs, tangled in a warm heap in the other bedroom. V. has perched himself on top, a contorted lump in a quilt. How easily I could creep in there, and take his hand, and lead him back here. Don't sleep there, I'd tell him. Sleep here.

I would die of embarrassment if he ever found this book.

But it's nice to have something to... I almost wrote 'live for.' But I mean 'enjoy oneself with,' don't I? I'm not staying alive for him, obviously. I am staying alive for me. But it isn't much fun, this whole staying alive business. You need to have a secret or two in wartime. Even if it is a war of attrition.

It's funny. We are a walled city, but the walls are five hundred years old, and crumbling. I fight with V. when he calls it a siege. To have a siege, I insist, you need to have walls. No, he says, you just need to have no way out; and anyway, we do too have walls.

Some walls. I can climb over them!

We watched, briefly, too frightened to laugh, as They tried to repair the low, crumbling walls when They first arrived, fumbling with the medieval stones like a drunk man with his keys. They seemed to have trouble making things stick together. I don't think that's why they've recruited human agents (or slaves or whathaveyou) but at any rate, the walls made no difference in the old days, and they make no difference now. When people are starved into submission, anything is a wall, because we are too weak to climb.

But he's right that there's a siege ring, and that since the Army abandoned us, it has quietly and completely closed. And he's right that there's no way out. The guards both day and night are not numerous, but they are <u>fast</u>, and they don't like people near the river, or the lake, or the train tracks, or the highway or bridges. If they see people moving there, they chase and harry us, or simply gather in their packs and attack, as if teaching us a lesson. One I've learned; I stay put, thank you.

I think of another famous siege, and I remember the Harvest Victory (ha! some name). But we didn't get that. We didn't get any warning, not a week, not a day, not even a minute. Just one second there was sky and sunset, and the next there was... Them.

In the movies, we would have seen Them on radar moving towards us through darkest ocean, through deepest space. Here, it was as if They stepped in from the other room. And everything came to an end.

Why here? Is there something special about here, our small city with its factories and its fields and its shoddy museums? We're nothing. We're a blister on the plain, surrounded by fields. Why do we not see Them in the distance, striding towards the mountains in the east?

The Army left us, anyway; they escaped the siege before it became a siege, not singing their songs. We who stayed fielded a new one. V. admitted soon after we met that he was a draft-dodger in this small, desperate second army. I'd guessed as much.

I was ashamed, he said. I thought you'd think less of me.

I do, I said, but I understand.

What a cruel thing to say, I thought even then, and I should have apologised or not said it at all, but we could not lie to each other; already we had survived too much.

Most everybody said yes to the recruiting squads. The few people that said no, my boys told me, were still dragged along to the shoddy training centres, in school auditoriums and the big stadium downtown. And then they went to defend the city. And they never came back.

So I never asked why. V. knew he would not come back.

No one knew anything about the missing children, not A., not B., not T1 and T2, who (being old women) usually know everything.

Alive? said A., fretfully. His eyes in that dark, wrinkled face seemed to recede some infinite distance, thinking perhaps, as we all were, of children we had known. Even I, who barely dare to say the names of my children even in my head.

At the market, said B. briskly. Someone will know.

Do you think so? I don't. But maybe when there's another one. I keep thinking, There's something I can do, there must be something. Why is everyone out there sleeping instead of combing the streets with me?

I ask this rhetorically. But. I'm so helpless and frustrated I'm shaking, I can't write. Even with my full stomach. I'm shaking.

I think of the boys, saying goodb

No. Think of something else. Sleep.

R<small>EPEATEDLY</small>, <small>QUIETLY</small>, <small>IRRITATEDLY</small>, Darian reminds me that I'm doing very different research from the three of them.

He hasn't said out loud that I don't belong on this trip—I got my funding same as they did, dammit—but he thinks it. And he keeps pointing out that aside from those first few triumphant days, we aren't finding evidence to really corroborate the things I find in the journal (which he keeps calling a 'diary'—and I don't know why it bothers me but it does).

And he's forbidden me, not in so many words, to continue asking the others for help.

He's right, though. They've all got their projects to complete, and we were only given twelve days here. Any time I take away for my own project has to be repaid, but they don't want what I've got to offer; as an anthropologist, they seem to think I'm essentially only useful to take notes, or as an extra pack bot.

Gloomily I feed Winnie's rats, scrub dirt out of her crawlers, sluice the smelly cleaning solvent through Victor's sampler heads. I feel hotly embarrassed in my silence that I came with no real tools except the document scanner. Look at you, Darian's silence seems to say, as they carefully perform routine maintenance on their tools at night. We came here to do real science, and you came to read a diary. Like a teenage girl. And maybe write a novel about it.

In penitence, or maybe just humiliation, I leave the journal alone during the day, and I tag along with the others as an extra body. Mostly Victor and Winnie, of course. The detection rats scamper ahead on their filament leads, their little silvery bodies blending smoothly into all the shattered concrete. "They used to use dogs," Winnie says as we follow them.

"Weird. How did they get into small spaces?"

"Right?"

Not very subtly, I steer us into the only reasonable spaces that it seems you could have staged a revolution. But even the drones and their LIDAR dongles cannot distinguish between the ordinary rubble and what might have been the mountain V. climbed up on. Wave your flag, I cry into the past. But of course, that's not *scientific*.

I beg the use of Darian's software to see if I can clean up the data and find a mountain, but after a couple of hours of the processor screeching and grinding, he comes over and grimly shakes his head. I haven't looked at the cleaned-up data yet. Where was their single, failed stand? Maybe I will never know.

I join Eva in her horror. Absolutely I am there with her and V. in that doorway, gasping for air. Kidnapping of children was hinted at but not confirmed in the few other primary documents. It was understood, it seemed, that children were both the most valuable thing in wartime and the hardest to keep safe. I wonder how old Eva's sons were, little I. and N.

The failure of the evacuation, I could have predicted that too. Diffidently, and couching it strictly in terms of data gathering offsite, I suggest that Winnie go check outside the city along likely routes; she agrees to send out the crawlers, but not her precious rats.

This could work. She wants the data too. I need to keep a closer eye out in the journal for things that could be useful to the others.

It's harder to focus now. There are things I desperately want to check, but don't want to go alone, and I can't ask the others. I'm getting paranoid that there are things still left in the city. Things? I don't know. I don't want to call them anything specific. There are certainly rats and mice. Maybe deer; you sometimes see leggy elegant things at night that turn and flee when they hear you. And you see their hoofprints, like posed droplets of water in the mud. What else lives here? Dogs? Wolves? Are wolves roaming this dead city? I mean, I know nothing can get into the pod, but still.

We're all having nightmares; no one talks about it. But you can hear it through the thin divisions, the sudden cessation of the long steady breath, then the snort, the gasp, the moan, the whimper. We all cry at night and in the morning we say 'God, this dust!' to explain our red eyes. Darian is snappish, short-tempered. In someone his size that's a little scary. I listened in while we got our seats calibrated for our flight here, and I think now: Okay, I'm not very good at math, but he is exactly twice as heavy as me.

I think: He wouldn't lay a finger on me.

I also think: Don't piss him off, though.

July 2

Couldn't go back to the old town today. I fret, I froth, I seethe.

Yet there are still miracles. It still seems like a miracle. I don't say V. himself. I mean: him, at my side, silently working, in the sun. It seems impossible that he is still here. When so much else has been taken from me.

Unwanted, unsummoned, this morning I looked at him peacefully eating his lunch out of a tin can and thought: <u>Is it for now or for always</u>. And it was a blow, a physical blow, as if an invisible fist had punched me right in the sternum; I think my heart even skipped a beat. I didn't want that line to appear.

I don't remember the rest.

<u>Is it for now or for always...</u>

That book that M. got me when we first started dating. No: before. Before either of us said anything, when we were friends, shy. But the whole book was love poetry in English. Shall I compare thee to a summer's day? he said, and I said, Only if I can compare you to a winter's day... And we laughed, not merely because we were so opposite, of course.

But he was, wasn't he? Looking at him was like the brightest, clearest day in February, when the ice was thick on the lake and you could throw New Year's parties on it, dine and dance on it, and you could see forever, all the way across the lake, to the far side of the globe, it seemed; everything about him was like that, clear and pure, like the crystal drops that fall from icicles.

I never told him that, of course.

And then coming home that day, when we thought the worst was past, the city was destroyed, the boys were gone, things stalked the street at night, that day, coming home alone into the cold flat where the fire had gone out, and he was gone, and there was nothing but an enormous red lace shawl on the wall, carefully pinned in a beautiful curved shape, and for a long time I did not even recognize what it was, till I noticed the dripping, still liquid, even still a little warm.

And I thought both: They left me nothing to bury, and: But that cannot be his blood. His is bright and clear. Like melted ice. Like a white, fair winter's day.

Nothing to bury. Nothing, I told myself, to mourn. Not like the boys. Maybe, I still find myself thinking, he is alive somewhere in the city, having lost both a tremendous amount of blood and his memory. Maybe he survived, and will find his way back to me one day; maybe they all will.

I don't know what else to mourn. You can't do it properly, it's all haphazard, in the five spare minutes you get between running, scrounging, fighting, guarding. My career? Can I say that died? I guess I won't get that back, so that's dead, yes. My home? Yes, that too. My plans to retire, to travel, to have a warm comfortable future? How trite. Those too. Add them to the list. My books, my clothes, whatever in the flat could burn in the bombings. Thank goodness we never had pets, I suppose.

I said goodbye to everything while running and that is not a proper goodbye.

July 10

Dreaming last night, those sickly half-dreams we all seem to get now, where you can see the wall and the glimmerings of the fire but you can't move or speak... we're close to death every day but I dreamed about the night I almost did die, and could never explain why I didn't.

We were out too late that night, we were caught in the open. I fell while the statue was chasing B. and A. and me and the others; I remember the fall but I didn't remember hitting my head, and indeed afterwards there was no mark, no blood in my hair, not even a headache, but I must have knocked myself out, I remember... I dreamt... consciousness swimming back through murky water, a layer of gray, a layer of white, a layer of black, then darkness, then focus. A square of starry sky. One eye open, the other glued shut with blood. The gap in my memory was brief but absolute.

But last night I remember: I stayed still. My body hummed with recent impact.

A bronze snout near me, passing inches from my unblinking eye. I thought: Don't blink. Of course, the overwhelming impulse is to do just that... but I held it back for long enough, and it moved on. Metal snout, hanging with iridescent tentacles like a catfish, a stench of greenblack breath, the eyes flat, clumsily cast, already cracked, apparently as unseeing as mine. But they can see.

And then the snout lifted, a flash of white crystalline teeth, a dangling black tongue. Since when do statues have tongues? And the legs moving past me, one two three four, all different lengths, in the shape of an X, so that it should have moved clumsily or at least unevenly, but it picked its way through the rubble and was gone.

I lay there, unmoving, listened for it to leave. It was a long time before the sound of its footsteps finally moved off. Perhaps as much as an hour. And other sounds... finishing off survivors. The choked-off gurgle, a hastily-ended scream. A bluish shimmer, as of a sudden reflection, like someone closing a car door. And then darkness again.

I awoke this morning with my heart pounding, clutching my chest. I slept in my jacket (the jacket of a dead man!). Maybe it opened something inside me, let something out. That memory, I had forgotten about that.

V. fussed over me when I came back in the middle of the night, and I let him. I was so tired. I had carried everything I could, painfully, step by step, often retreating into buildings, stopping to touch my bloodless head.

What was it? he said.

I don't know, I told him.

I couldn't remember. But now I do.

It's not just that, as we said in those first days, They're something that we hadn't discovered before. The ocean is full of strange things, people said stubbornly. Or maybe They beamed down from a superior civilization.

But close to, I felt the true explanation was neither of those things. Nothing so prosaic as something that evolved, that lived in a place and made a place its home. I felt intensely, if inaccurately, seeing that thing up close, that They are not from here, in any sense, <u>any</u>, that a human mind would understand as 'here.' Nowhere is 'here' for Them. Or everywhere is here. They stepped through from somewhere else, I am sure of it.

And maybe that's why my mind knocked me out again, trying to protect me before I thought the inevitable next thing, because there it was: We cannot live with these things. We cannot fight Them. We are not on the same level as these things. Maybe They are not all-knowing, or all-powerful, but They are similar enough to gods that we are doomed. We, as not just humans but mortals, are doomed. There will be no resistance except in our minds. And maybe They can see that too, and will root it out and end it.

We will never know Them because we cannot know Them.

I hear thin screams sometimes, in different neighbourhoods. And I rush to empty buildings, warehouses, schools, expecting to find—what? A room full of captive children? But I know the cries of children and how they differ from adults, and I know I'm hearing them. What can I do, where are they? I am torn between giving up looking for them and thus losing what few shreds of sanity I have left, and enlisting the entire city in the search.

It has occurred to me (O cynical Eva!) that They have learned to mimic the cries of children, the way the ravens near my work used to imitate the coughs of smokers outside, and are... what? Luring me into a trap?

No, V. would say, if he were here. They're like wasps.

But some wasps are intelligent, you know. I read it somewhere. I don't know. If we're talking about intent, that statue with the little boy, it had intent. Or even Intent, capital I. And it is a war. And terrible things happen to children in war.

Give up? Press on?

CAN'T SLEEP, CAN'T sleep, can't work, can't sleep.

A strange thing. The camera film I found in the museum, a single dropped roll in the corner by the door, buried in a little snowdrift of dirt and broken glass, was confirmed by my scanner to be intact and undeveloped. And precious, of course—by the time the Invasion occurred, practically nobody was using film cameras. But someone at this museum had one. I'm sure it's nothing more than shots of the statues and the grounds outside. But I checked it again this morning and the film is corrupted, blurred, as if some kind of... fungus or spore has grown on it. Just in the couple of days. I'm stunned, horrified. Maybe once I get it back to the university lab I will be able to recover it.

But I wonder now: Are there lingering effects in these siege cities? Is there something still here, like an echo, screwing things up? Maybe it's the film. Maybe it's the scanner. Maybe it's both. I should see if the others are experiencing anything like that.

Early this morning I sleepwalked and sort of got fixated on the constellations over us, before the sun came up, and nearly fell off my concrete block, which I was barely aware I had climbed. Winnie rescued me. I said, "What are you doing here?" and she said "I can't remember." We stared at each other for a minute. So awkward.

Even now I think: That can't be what Eva meant, that 'pull,' can it? God. What have we gotten ourselves into? That's never happened at any of my other research sites.

Under Darian's quiet, relentless pressure, every day now I debate changing my research route, rewriting my project plan. Something harder. More scientific. What kind of thesis am I going to have at the end of this? A fluffy romance novel, like Darian says. Maybe I should surrender the diary to someone else so they can work with it when I get back. I mean, it's only a once in a lifetime chance, with limited funding, in an area that surprisingly few places are willing to sponsor, that's all. I might never be able to come back here and check all the details. That's all. If people are figuring out what happened to the world, of course they need numbers, measurements, graphs, charts, statistical analyses, and those horrible black-and-white photos of broken metal that Darian takes with his laser ruler that give me a headache to look at.

I'll never be able to come back here and maybe that's for the best. Let that money go to the others, I don't know.

I'm concerned at the mention of 'joining.' Will Eva or V. knuckle under? I suppose I shouldn't care. Whoever they are, they died a long time ago.

And yet, I do care, I can't help it. It's torture to not know. What would I have done? I ask myself, but it's an unanswerable question; the world we live in is not the world they, or They, lived in.

I find myself sick with the suspicion that they both died before the end of the Setback. And they never even knew it was so close. That all they had to survive was about another year.

The Army did abandon them, of course; I secretly dug in Darian's data and found a ton of drone flight data over the sunflower fields outside the walls, and buried military detritus. Some of it is so close that if we leave out one side of the city we could walk for five minutes and climb directly into a tank. But I'm not doing that on my own. Anyway, it would require me to admit I've been snooping. Absolutely not.

I looked up the whole poem that Eva referenced this morning and now I find myself on a rooftop, sitting alone, while the others poke and scrape below on their various pursuits. These people, we know in our heads that they were real, and whole, and had hopes and dreams and goals and visions. But how cruel of us, how thoughtless, to not see them as real people, and not just primary sources, till we find something like this. I wish I could find the flat with the blood on the wall, but it would take forever to search.

Winnie and I fight about this sometimes. Her methods are mostly noninvasive, and leave everything in the ground after the scan, but sometimes she digs up bones and puts them in jars, and we look at each other defiantly. Those bones are going for analysis. They won't come back here for burial. We rob the dead, and we say, "Well, that's research for you," but... the husband's death, that lacy shawl of blood on the wall. Nothing was left for Eva to bury.

I'm so upset. I don't know what I can do. Maybe at the end of the trip, I will put the book back where I found it—I still have the plastic bags, the cinderblock it rested in. I have the full scan, after all, which does isotope and chemical analysis and is in some ways better than the book. But still. I cradle it to me, I touch the delicate old pages, I sniff it hungrily. It's over a hundred years old, this book. It means something to me to be able to touch it. But perhaps I shouldn't be touching it. The others wouldn't understand.

I'm confused, still, about the statues. All the other primary sources are no help either. Is the bronze they always speak of (sometimes brass, iron, copper, stone) the metal, or the colour, or both? Who made the statues? Are they robots or automatons of some kind, programmed by the Invaders to keep Their order in the cities? I simply cannot understand 'comes alive at night,' but everyone said it, and most people saw it once or twice and survived.

July 14

Still searching. Went out first thing at dawn, after a night of screaming, nightmares, and unseasonal, awful aurora. Filling the whole sky, like a silk scarf. Roar and chant and burn and howl from constellations whose names I've never known.

I admit (don't tell V.) that I felt the pull again, and nearly toppled out the window. Snatched the sill at the last moment, and cut my fingers on the broken glass. I still hear it, that thin, high whine from the stars. I don't dare look even long enough to try to figure out which constellation it might be (how clear they all are now!). I want to open the shutters and bellow <u>Fuck off!</u>

God, can you imagine.

Endlessly, as if performing penitence, I think about that child, dangling in the brass jaws of the statue. When I find myself not thinking about him, I force myself back to it.

From all those science fiction movies I knew: People took to the road to get away from the end of the world, and they found new communities together, and eventually things got better. Not like this, pinned down, terrified, exhausted, in a world no one can understand. Where all the rules are broken and no one is coming for us.

I miserably confess that I think more about that dangling child than I think about my own boys. Both memories are raw wounds, but one is so deep and welling with pain that I feel that I cannot even touch it, lest, like a broken bone, something shift and puncture me and I bleed out on the floor at the thought of it. (They're all right. They're together. They're all right. I have to keep telling myself.)

I should never have let the boys go. I should never have let them go.

I know they would have gone no matter what I said, but... I could have tried harder.

And they went with so much unsaid, so much not even hinted at. That they barely knew my own parents before the accident, that I was plunged so deeply into grief that M. parented all alone for almost a year, I never apologised for that. They were old enough to hear it. And grieving for their grandparents too, poor little things.

I tell myself it was all right, that losing my parents wasn't the same disaster for them as it was for me. The boys had each other, and they had M. And I had myself... if we are being honest, here on this thin paper, on which my pencil might glide like a confessional whisper, if we are, I had begun to fret, already, even though they were perfectly healthy (God forgive me) about Mama and Papa moving into the flat with us, that the day would come when they could not manage stairs in that huge ridiculous house any more, that one day inevitably on the phone I'd say, Why don't you just come live with us? and it would be the end of whatever little life, whatever little personality, remained in myself, that I would be pulled too many ways...

And then the world ended and the veil dropped from my eyes and I saw that yes, I was always mediocre, as daughter, student, wife, mother, friend, employee. That I was dull and dutiful and the girl who laughed at poetry and chased the boys on the frozen lake was not actually dead and gone, as the cliché would have it, but buried alive, and still screaming, quietly, under the monumental weight of grown-up responsibilities. And now I only have one—to survive.

Can I do any better?

I don't know.

It is infuriating that I have turned out to be one of those Mad Max people, a born survivor, impossible to kill; I have watched in despair as people stronger, bigger, faster, smarter, luckier than me died or were killed or starved. I shouldn't be here, but here I am.

I wish I weren't. Oh God! That little boy, alive in the mouth of the monster.

What can I do?

I am <u>so angry</u> at the Army for abandoning us, I am so betrayed. I never thought of it in those words before. I thought, at the time: Well, of course they are going outside the wall to fight. Only then can they turn to the ones in the city, which are fighting guerilla style and killing thousands every day. They are being resupplied from the outside. If we were not cut off, we could be rescued; we learned that from the failed evacuation, in which everyone was massacred down to the last flea.

But now I think: You Army bastards stole my children

and vanished and I bet you did not even fight one day. I bet you deserted. Fled into the countryside. Well, joke's on you. The only place you can live now is a city.

Except that you have my boys, you bastards. You took my <u>boys</u>.

July 17

We shopped well yesterday and today a girl named Polina joined our furtive community dinner. The first question we ask ourselves is: Is this person an agent? We didn't use to, but there are so many of them now. More every day. I hear of the squads roaming the cities, killing agents or trying to, and dispersing quickly, like roaches, to avoid retaliation from the statues; but the agents also roam, and kill.

I suppose that's all right, to kill people who are trying to kill you. But privately I think I would also kill a traitor if I knew one, whether he was trying to kill me or not.

There are spies now. But there should be no sympathisers. None.

With that said, she does not seem the type. She does not seem as if she has ever submitted to any authority in her life, even the ones at the university where she says she was studying. She is a small fast-moving teenager who reminds me inexplicably of a dark gray tabby cat, or just a kitten, wearing an oversized leather jacket with a giant American flag on the back over her ripped leggings, as top-heavy as an ice cream cone. She bolted her food, even the horrible sardines, and I thought of the boys doing the same thing, not deigning to chew, and I

These Lifeless Things

closed my eyes for a long time, barely hearing her and V. speaking.

V. said, It's all bullshit, you know. Our enemy is endless, numberless, and the resources They can muster are infinite.

Says who? snapped the girl.

I saw, he said, before the electricity went. There were news reports all over the world. Thousands and thousands of Them, pouring through the holes They made in the bend of things, and behind Them, you could see thousands more. They will always be here. They will always rule us.

And I was stunned. He never told me he thought that. That we were defeated no matter what we do.

But now, sitting here in the warm room while the rain falls outside, I think: Do I think that too?

I was never beautiful, never popular. It seemed like a joke that I ended up with the life that lined up so closely to the one I wanted: the house full of light and noise, the husband with his clear, pure eyes, the doors banging open and shut. I hated being alone. I'm alone all the time now. Even with V. next to me, I feel alone. As if the appearance of the Them cut through the laws of physics and space and time and gravity and... and whatever holds people together, rather than molecules. I look at people I've known for two years and I think: I don't know you at all; who are you?

And yet: what a selfish thing to think about the end of the world.

I just want to live. I'll kill to live. V. is just like that, a small carnivorous creature just like me. Falcon, stoat, fox. Not lion or bear. Nothing so big and unwieldy, but a little awful dangerous thing that kills in silence, and alone. We move through the world killing and trying to kill and that's all we do now.

I had dreams once, I think, of doing or being something else. All hazy now. I liked our tiny garden, liked coaxing vegetables and flowers from the earth, identifying and tearing out weeds, brushing bees off my cheeks; I liked picking mushrooms when we went camping, the swing of the axe, the gentle and domestic danger of picking apples. Life was small and safe and I saw it through a pinhole. I thought I would be a short fat baba one day with an apron full of treats. I had never been out in the world, never known the breadth and length of it. I suppose I never will now.

SHE SPEAKS OF solar storm and abnormal auroral activity, but there's no way to measure it now. I made the mistake of mentioning it to Darian, in case he knew of some obscure method I'd never heard of, and he said I'd just have to rely on my hand-me-down stories, because there was no way of measuring it. "But we can predict it," I said weakly, "can't we sort of figure out a pattern for the—" and he said, "Emerson, we have telescopes trained on the sun, not the past."

The big telescopes couldn't be used back then. As soon as anyone figured out how to get the lights on again, or even tried to turn on a phone, they found the full attention of Them directed on them, irritated, irrational, irregular, and whatever device had managed to power itself up would have five minutes to an hour before it died again, normally with its unlucky operators. Long enough to field some bombers, if you didn't mind the 100 percent fatality rate for the pilots rather than their targets, of whom the fatality rate seemed to be zero, inasmuch as you couldn't tell whether you'd killed any of Them. All Eva would have thought was: bombers are still in the air. Can't they rescue us? No.

I'm so sorry. No.

July 19

The sentinels seem to have lost interest in old town, or maybe our smells are just less fresh and irritating to them after the days of rain; today I insisted that V. and Polina come back with me and look properly.

We should split up so we can cover more ground, V. said, and I agreed at first; we took paint sticks and scribbled marks on all the buildings we checked. Very Biblical of us, P. said. But after a few hours, hearing invisible things move around in the rubble, we rejoined, silently, a little contrite. There's safety in numbers, and the three of us might be able to join our tired, half-starved forces to beat something up that we couldn't alone.

V. is useless with directions. I made sure we didn't double back. The trees craned to watch us, as they do, and even some of the shrubs; P. gave them an unusually wide berth.

One of them tried to grab me, she muttered. A while back. A topiary actually. In the rich part of town.

Some of them, more worryingly, are developing what appear to be... I don't want to say teeth, or beaks, or both, but their branches are becoming something like chainsaws, with clear sharp items growing from the twisted bark like broken glass from a beer bottle. And they are changing colour; the bark is no longer gray or brown or dotted with lichen, but dusky violet and bronze. Luckily that makes them easy to spot, and we keep our weapons up, by our faces, as we're forced to pass by.

I've tried to kill the statues during the day, P. said as we passed a particularly large specimen, as high as the hotel it stood next to, riddled with cracks and already turning green in the damp air.

Us too, said V. I think everyone has.

She said, Yeah? I used a gun. A shotgun. Like for ducks? And there wasn't even a sound until it hit the building behind of it. The bullets just passed right through. It's like they're not even real during the day.

We paused for a moment and looked at it. I tried to picture what it looks like at night, when they come alive. It was too big, I couldn't do it.

The ground is littered with the prints of the sentinels and the local statues, though. They're around this area a lot. Something is happening here, something is up. The few people we saw shrugged when we asked them though.

Have you seen children around here? I pressed. Maybe with statues or sentinels? Maybe with agents?

No, they all said, staring at me, hard. No children. There are no children in this city.

As far as I can tell, they're right, and they're wrong. There are none now, but there was one.

* * *

July 22

Whispers, murmurs today. A surreptitious and near-spontaneous market, like the others in courtyards, on rooftops, in side-streets where everyone can run if they need to. These are the only places where I can see faces different from the faces I see all the time—V., P., A., the handful of others in my neighbourhood. We meet briefly and our eyes rove hungrily over strange faces, we seek novelty now.

Someone whispered, There's a town I heard of. Where people are fighting back against Them.

I lunged, I dropped my basket; behind me, V. cursed.

Where did you hear that, I said. An old man, a dishonest face, shifty. Look at you, you liar, I wanted to say. You were lying long before the invasion—what were you? You lied for a living, whatever it was. An insurance adjustor or something.

I said, Tell me the name of the town.

He said, That, I don't know. But not far. Not even a hundred kilometers west. Soon, we'll see the fires in the night sky, all the colours of Their bodies burning.

They don't have bodies, P. said.

Their servants, the old man said stubbornly, looking between me and her. And Their agents. And the statues...

You can't burn the statues, I said, and turned, but he had already seen the hunger in my eyes; I saw it too, reflected back in his, and I stayed, defiant, I did not want him to think he had driven me off. Funny colour, kind of a greeny-yellow. Who else did they say had eyes like a lynx?

I said, How? You tell me that.

He said, Never mind how. Someone figured out how to turn Their bad magic against 'em. You'll see the fires, and then you'll know.

Who told you? P. said, her little tabby claws out. He took a step back. The market was breaking up, the sky too; we had to get home before dark.

People who know, the old man said.

You mean agents, P. said. That's who you've been talking to. They lie, they've got a job to do. Why do They need agents? That's for humans. What are the agents doing, what are they administering?

The old man looked at me then, and said, Watch this one, eh? She asks too many questions.

He melted into the shadows like a movie vampire, and P. and I looked at each other; I know <u>you're</u> not an agent, I wanted to tell her. You were asking all the same questions I wanted to ask.

Come on, she said. We'd better go.

Grateful to her for that, but I keep thinking about it. We spoke for perhaps two minutes and really, truly, we learned nothing useful. But my whole body is on fire tonight, thinking about it. I feel as if, were I to go outside in the rain, it would blast off me in steam before it even hit my skin.

I am furious, pinioned, I want to know more—my hands clench as I write, see how I dig into the paper. Tell me! Tell me! Goddamn you! Why can they fight and we cannot? Why are we trapped and dying here? What secret do they know? Where are the children of that town? Where are their children? And where are ours? It isn't fair!

V. is sleeping on the floor; can he hear the book rattle against the table? I am trying to write quietly, but I'm going too fast. I suppose tomorrow I won't be able to read this. Trying to save my candle. I'm so angry. I should have dragged the old man down an alleyway and found out what he knew. P. would have helped me.

The way V. looks at her... I feel uneasy, then irritated at myself. She's a pretty young woman, and he's young too, and if they want to look at each other any way they want, they should. I've got no skin in the game either way. But they still look. And I still watch them looking. Wish I could stop. I have other things I need to think about. The heart beats on as if it intends to live, as if it deserves to do so, even if it can't come up with a reason why.

July 23

Fucking traitors! How they creep amongst us, like cockroaches disguised as our neighbours. That old man, I knew it.

Shaking. Can't write.

Later

Ambushed and attacked while we were out. Not by the usual. By a mob of humans, silent, their faces covered.

And in broad daylight, blue sky. It was so strange to see a group of people now that for a second I stopped, startled, and V. had to leap in.

We couldn't run, it was far too late. Ended up fighting them off by the absolute skin of our teeth. I badly injured one, leaving him in the street, and the others ran. I think: They weren't sent to kill us, just incapacitate us. Stop them, someone said. They ask too many questions. Even though we have all discovered just how easy it is to kill someone. How delicate the human body really is.

They knew where to find us. We'll have to move flats now. That's what I get for getting attached to this one. I could kick myself.

V. said, We're onto something.

I agreed. Told him this was the most important thing we could be doing now.

He said, Oh, you're on a mission now. You think you've found something to live for. A 'purpose' in life.

I don't know why, but I got so angry for a second that I could barely see. Maybe it was just the obviousness of it. Maybe it was... I don't know. I flew into a rage, I almost slapped him; I drew my hand back.

I said, If you think that's laughable, then you're a fucking coward. That's what you are. Laugh at it, then. Laugh. So we know what you are.

And you're a hypocrite, he said. You told me your only goal was survival, that everyone's only goal now was survival. And now you go and change your tune because your ovaries hurt or because you want people to think you're a hero or whatever. As if there will be history books later for children to read.

I did slap him then, and while we were both still reeling, I said, Everyone's only goal _is_ survival now. And that means we all make sure everyone survives.

He stared at me, his cheek reddening. A little drool of blood from the corner of his mouth. I was startled by the blood, remorseful; I didn't think I hit him that hard. I've never slapped anyone before.

I said, So go on. Abandon me then. If you have a mission of your own. Some better mission. As if the reasons we're doing something matter so much to you, as if any reason could be better than any other reason.

No, he said. I want to help.

Because you can't think of anything better to do with your life, I said.

I suppose so, he said.

We went to sleep after that, exhausted, in separate rooms, as usual. It was the most awkward thing in the world. But we're not giving up.

August 1

Exhausted. Can barely move. Bleeding seems to have stopped though. Should have attempted stitches tonight, but disoriented; couldn't see. Will unwrap it and try tomorrow.

Bedroom door shut tight, barricaded with a bookshelf. Glad I brought a flashlight. The stranger sleeps outside, uneasily, groaning and struggling on the floor before falling again into silence. No flashlight for him; the statues roam outside, they might see his light. Not so mine, in this windowless room. Well, anyway, the sound means he's alive.

The classic mistake. I've seen this in the movies too. The stranger rescued, fulsome in his gratitude. Infiltrates the greater group and then turns out to be... some kind of traitor or cannibal or zombie or something. But what the movies never adequately show is that you cannot leave them to die, you just cannot. Something in you wants to, and you turn to go, and then it's as if your skeleton turns, your muscles turn, while your gaze stays fixed in the middle-distance.

Humanity! I think it only as a curse now. It's my bane, my enemy, it comes at me in waves, like labour pains, all those years ago; the world ended and I see it again as if recognizing an old enemy on the far side of the street. You! I hiss, between the waves, in the troughs, gasping for breath. You again! And it is also, besides enemy, foe, loathed one, the only thing I think I can still love. I am otherwise dead inside, numb as stone. I look inside myself and see a paleness where others have rich red blood, or pure sunshine and ice; no, never mind the stuff that seeps through the bandages now. Spoiled milk. Light shines into me and is eaten immediately and eagerly by the dark.

Bloody, awful humanity! I saw him scrabbling over the broken stones, cutting his hands and wrists, not crying out for help; we never do that now, it's not wise, it only attracts things. For a second I froze. The thing after him was huge, twisted; in fact, it looked a bit like it had survived a fall from a building, and was in that death posture, twisted and curled, but it could still run. When you have twenty or thirty legs you do not miss a handful. It skittered after him over the rocks, screeching, followed by its entourage, all fangs and eyes. The worst ones I've ever seen.

And then I unfroze, and picked up my hoe.

It was a short fight; they tend to be. The statues are numerous and malevolent and dangerous but they are shoddily made, and they can be immobilized, if not killed; a dozen rapid blows of the hoe had its head half-off, and then it reared, disoriented, and fell upon its followers, and we swatted them away as we ran for it. One of them clawed me, deep, bad. Yet I still held him up as we found this place, darted up the stairs, shut the firedoors behind us. The rest of the world called it Brutalism, this blocky concrete stuff; now, after the end of things, we call it Utilitarianism. Because it's useful, see—well, that's not fair. Being a brute is useful too, now.

I taped him up, asked him his name, didn't understand his answer. Went in here and shut the door. His eyes in their round masks of blood were luminous, grey-blue, a small white flame burning behind each pupil like the reflection of the sun in a bottomless lake. I know nothing about him except this.

And something else, something that makes me unnecessarily uneasy, because it's... it's a big city, and there must be warehouses, storehouses, caches, other things I don't know about, but everyone now, two years post-Invasion, is like a scarecrow, skinny and tough, and light enough to sling over your shoulder. But he, the stranger, is very, very heavy. Not merely muscular but bulky. Like M. Solid, big bones and over that, the dense good flesh that we all used to boast about, even as models and actors grew skinnier and skinnier.

I don't want to say it, but.

What has he been eating?

My flashlight dims. Can They affect that even here? Do I write so slowly now? I will write more tomorrow, if we are alive.

Something stalks up the stairs, metal against concrete. If that thing phases into this room through one of those weird tears in the air it is going to get an extraordinarily heavy tactical flashlight jammed down its gullet. Leave us alone for one goddamn night, goddamn you!

August 2

Woke this morning to find the man still alive, glued to the rug with dried blood. I unstuck him and shook him awake.

My name is... Konstantin, he said, and I thought: Good, then you can go into my diary, because your name does not start with the same letter as anyone else's. We did not wait for the other names. No one gives them any more.

He thanked me. I accepted his thanks. I didn't know what else to say.

I did not say, Stay here in this neighbourhood, with everyone else. Out loud, I said, I expect you'll have people to get back to.

He said, No. Not any more.

Ah, I said.

Rude to pry. Especially when the answers were all

around us for a while, rotten and mummified, grasping each other in their last desperate moments, like the ash casts from Pompeii; so many that we stopped seeing them till they began to vanish, so many that we never could bury nor burn them, though of course, in those early months, we did try. He must remember that.

I told him, There are a few of us, and we are getting by. If you help us, we'll feed you.

All right, he said. Thank you.

But we have to rest today.

Yes, he said. What can I do? Your leg doesn't look good. Can I get water? Wood?

So I sent him out an hour ago to scavenge for cans and water and whatever else, and when he was gone I heated up the needle I keep in my collar and stitched the worst parts of the claw wound shut. Unsanitary, I suppose, using that curtain thread. But I've got a good immune system, and there was lots of it, the thread I mean, unravelling easily from the clumsy hemming job someone did at the bottom. When M. and I first moved out, we had curtains like that, and he never knew how bad a job I had done at shortening them for the window. Things to remember, things to forget. Leg is propped stiffly in front of me now, which makes a good desk to balance this book on.

VICTOR AND I pick things up with tweezers and put them in jars, plastiseal them in clear packets, like pills, to analyze later. There seems to be something different about this than Winnie with her bones, and me with my words. We seem like vampires or ghouls or something, while

Victor seems like a real scientist, dreamy, focused, pure. I sometimes find myself resenting that he never has to deal with our moral dilemmas of consent, theft, desecration of the dead. He leans down and snips seedlings, and hands them to me to embed in the bags of clear nutrient gel. (It tastes like coconut. We've all sneaked a bit; it was that or die of curiosity.) "Soon, we'll have siege trees growing back home," I said, and he nodded, excited.

There's such a thing as the love of truth, I think, watching him handle the seedlings so gently, watching Winnie's hands on her bone fragments, far more delicate than any manipulator on even the most carefully-engineered drone. But if that's true then truth can come in many forms; as many as love.

Victor hands me a seedling and says, "People always misunderstand 'survival of the fittest.' Even now. It doesn't mean we rush over each other to the exits to survive. It means we help each other become more fit. There's the micro-level of you, your genes, which you want to live above all others. But then there's also the macro level. Not of you or even your family, but your species, your ecosystem."

I nod absently. The seeds and even nuts we pick up are sometimes disquietingly serrated, all razor-sharp edges and clear patches. Victor tells me they're quite normal and will lend no credence to them ever 'grabbing' people. But his genetic analyses show that where you'd normally find ordinary elm or linden seeds or the occasional chestnut, something has 'obviously' modified them. "Maybe a gall," he says, and we don't meet each other's eyes. "Or some other parasite. Maybe a fungus."

I think Darian is sabotaging my investigation. I can't say anything. Baseless suspicions, nothing you could hang your hat on, and the others would roll their eyes at me. He got the vast majority of the funding for this trip, he usually calls the shots. He's the reason we got a real research pod instead of a crappy trailer, he's the one who made sure that we could charter a hover to drop us out here instead of schlepping everything in by truck and foot.

At any rate, no matter what he's doing, it continues. The investigation, I mean. In my off-hours I still tack around the city, mazed with wonder and terror, trying to confirm the things I find in Eva's journal.

The student, Polina, says you can't hit the statues during the day with a shotgun? I've never seen that before. "Applied science," I said last night during dinner, and Darian said "What?" and I flung a rock at the one near our pod. It hit, solidly, and ricocheted off the faceted bronze surface to land somewhere in the darkness. The sound was unbelievable, a deafening gong like I'd hit a churchbell. We stared at it in absolute childish horror for a moment, as if that were its cue to 'come alive' and attack us, but of course nothing happened.

I found a place to hide and read the journal, the real version, while I lie and tell the others that I'm with someone else, when I can't bear it any more. Another research team, I read on my notepad, is headed to a town about a hundred klicks away at the end of the month. I wonder if it's the one where people fought back. But how do you tell?

My secret place has ancient candles everywhere, imprisoned in clear glass and brass lanterns or bare on marble shelves, lighting the huge decorated room like a Renaissance painting of the annunciation. I wonder what it used to be, once. Not a church. To get in you pass through a place so small that I had to put my bag in front of me to fit through the doorway, arched black brick. Here and there marked with scarlet, as if the brick itself were not black but plain red and had once been burned. Down several uneven steps into a low room, brushing past silk scarves and gloves, lipstick displays, antique compacts, feather fans, silver filigree card holders. And three shelves of perfumes, thick glass slabs on brass fittings, then the door into the bigger room. Maybe it was a store. But what a store! I light the candles, poke out bricks for ventilation. I don't want the others to find me in here, dead from bad air.

There *are* history books, Eva. Children are still being taught. And we are the descendants of the people you rescued.

I need to ask Winnie about the nutritional states of the bones she's finding, I know she can do that analysis. Were they well-fed or starving? If we find some wonderfully well-fed bones, the bones of a glutton, would those be Konstantin's bones? I wonder. I must break myself of the habit of thinking that any of these people can be identified. Only their traces are left.

August 27

K. works in the garden, uncomplaining. His hands look all right, don't they? We noticed in that skirmish that Their agents, the thralls I'm convinced have been deputized to administer Their reign on Earth, had been issued official badges, horrible, insectile things with razor edges. I am quite sure they move when you're not looking. But at any rate: you know an agent because of their bloodied handkerchiefs and raw fingertips. I suppose he could still be working with them, unofficially. What spy would blow his cover with such an obvious thing as his hands?

He talks while he works. About revolution, about counter-revolution, about trains filled with doomed royalty. These things, he had told people again and again in those first dark weeks, never changed; you could read about it in the textbooks, write papers about it, even teach it, but until you lived it, you could not expect to truly understand. And that was why they survived.

This man is not old enough to have their attitude—courtly but adamantine. He is some kind of scholar. But he will not talk about his past. Not unusual in and of itself; many don't. It is a monumental kind of pain, like birth, and despite what my mother told me, unforgettable; you do not do it more than is necessary. To keep with the comparison, such a large thing as one's comfortable, safe past in the city, fed and warm, with one's family still alive, cannot pass through such a small orifice as the mouth.

I think sometimes of all the things I have not told V.

About my boys, for one. I am terrified he will recognize their names and he will turn out to have attended their school or something. About M., yes; but not his death. Not even my last name, nor he his; no one does now, as K. knows. As if our families, gone, can carry those names only; as if we the living must get by with something else, as if only in death are the names truly safe. I only half-disbelieve it. They can take everything including all the blood from a body and all the spirit too, all the memories, intelligence, all the heat, all the veins, all the hair and nails; we've all seen it; who's to say They cannot take a name?

Anyway, to admit it would be to also admit that I took Mariusz' name when we married. So I am no better than Them. That I took it out of love would make no difference. They don't know what love is anyway.

I hate that my leg is still sore. No infection yet. Just the tired, angry ache of ripped muscle and whatever godawful things live on the feet of those little monsters, healing. If I were twenty years younger, if I were V.'s age, I would be walking this off already.

No one speaks of the missing children while we search, while we interrogate, while we mark the buildings. No one speaks: but we think about it all the time.

If I asked K. about it, I wonder what he would say. But he is still too new to trust with this fragile thing that we do not, ourselves, know what to do with. He is not really a part of this neighbourhood. I'll ask V. about him later. Maybe even P., who senses (I think) that I am not really at ease around her, but (I am quite, quite sure) does not know why.

It grieves me to see it in her eyes, she is so hungry for love and connection, and so angry about that need within herself that she kills it every day, she stamps down on its corpse, it is buried in a cast-iron coffin at her personal crossroads. I would give her all that love so easily, if not for this one juvenile, awful thing. I hate myself for it. She can never know. Yes, I'll talk to her too. I could give her this one thing. I give so little now.

September 15

We search; we still have to eat. Have to feed the grief, or else what will it eat in its hunger? We are breaking new ground now, for what we would have probably once referred to as patriotism gardens or victory gardens but now we do not even call them gardens, we just call them food; we are breaking new ground for food, a fall planting. At the outskirts of the old park near the cemetery, where several huge trees were torn down on Invasion Day, the ground has been reclaimed by weeds and concrete bits; but it's a good location, I've been scouting it for a while.

We heaped up a guard tower, and put V. on it while A. and P. and K. and I did the digging for most of the day. Things flitted in the treetops, though not for long; every now and then something would shoot out, and there would be a brief cry, and a flurry of feathers. Soft, soft grey or iridescent violet, like clouds.

The pigeons all left, P. said, looking up, alertly, and baring her kittenish teeth at the trees. Then they were coming back.

Were, I said.

I hate these trees, she said.

Me too. We couldn't go any deeper into the park; we'd be torn apart. Things live there during the day, and walk freely in the tentacled shadows of the ancient trunks, just as the statues walk in the night.

We'll probably be all right here in the open, I said.

The soil was black and safe, and familiar, and curiously uncontaminated. K. said, We have some of the best soil in the world, you know. Make a dead stick bloom.

I hope so. There are fewer of us to be fed, but there will be more if we get the children out. Where are they, where have they been taken? Is it shameful of me to feel proud for putting seedlings in rows? I should be storming the Bastille of Monsters, dammit.

Think of them in there.

I can't think of anything but! How am I supposed to stay alive, thinking like that?

They say: You put on your own oxygen mask first, and then you tend to others. But remember when we were flying for that choir competition and the plane dropped and I snatched at the mask and put it over I.'s face, and M. just looked at me, from behind his own... you're meant to put on your own mask first. You can't help others unless you help yourself.

But have I gotten too used to helping myself? I don't know. I hate my mind sometimes; I wish I could turn it off, as in the old days.

One worrying thing. When V. and P. switched spots on the guard tower, she lasted all of an hour before standing, calling out, garbled words, no language any of us knew. We all spun, expecting to see sentinels approaching, slithering over the fresh black soil, emerging from the trees. We were ready to fight. But no, it was just the girl, her head thrown to the sky, this unbelievable stream of noise from her mouth, trying to speak Their language, the one we hear in dreams. V. seemed glued to the spot in sheer terror. K. panicked. A. sighed, and hefted his shovel.

You stay away from her! I shouted, and scrabbled up the heap of stones we'd built to the flat spot on top, and grabbed the girl's leather jacket, pulling her nearly on top of me; for a second we teetered, startled, in the sunlight, gasping for air. But she stopped the noise as soon as I touched her, and I knew it was one of those... moments, just a moment, we all get them. Mostly while we sleep, when we can't hurt ourselves. Sometimes, admittedly, during the day.

She was shamefaced afterwards, quiet. She dug and picked rocks without complaint, her eyes and nose swollen and red, as if she was about to cry, but would not permit herself to do so. Something, perhaps her abruptly cut-off call, attracted small ugly sentries from the neighbourhood that harried us whenever we lowered our heads, and were driven off with the chunks of rubble that we dug from the dark dirt.

Don't be upset, I told her as we walked back. Nothing happened.

I kept hearing things, she muttered. Singing. From the sky. I followed it... but that was months ago. I thought it stopped.

It's all right, I said.

And then she did cry, clenching her jaw against it, angry at herself. She swiped at her face with her dirty hands and left rich black smears. I ignored it, she said. I didn't... I didn't listen to the...

I said, Listen. Whatever secret knowledge They brought with Them, it is not for us, not really. They will say that it is because They will say anything to have Their way with this world. How do you think They get agents? But you didn't fall for it.

No, she said. I didn't.

I can't believe, looking back, how fast I climbed up that rock tower, nearly splitting my stitches. To shut her up, I told myself. Because the noises people make can attract all sorts of things. It's a sign, it's like a spell; it tells Them that something worked. I did it because I wanted to live.

You can live with anything. You can live as anything. It always comes to an end, and then afterwards, you can say: I did what I had to, and I lived to tell the story. I bear witness, even though to do so I had to do some terrible things.

Leg mostly healed. Will it slow me down, later?

Where are the fireworks we were promised?

I HAVE TO find that park. How many old parks near cemeteries are there with big trees torn down? I found a very likely candidate on the drone imagery, but I can't find the guard tower. There *are* a lot of pigeons here, though. And magpies, which we have back home, but not so tamely brash. In particular they like Victor, and follow him around not wheedling scraps but keeping up a burbling commentary as if they are trying to explain what happened to the trees. The genetic memory of corvids: they're supposed to be smart, aren't they? I wonder what they remember. What they've passed down.

The soil is still good here; even I can see that. Soft, crumbly, not dark brown but black, as black as asphalt. Privately I pocket a bagful of it, and some of Victor's weird seeds, as we walk. Maybe I will grow them in my little apartment when I get back home next week.

At the candidate park I think I see some evidence of cultivation, not just the ground broken but furrows still remaining, but it's so muddled from the decades of weeds and neglect and saplings pushing up that it's hard to tell. Instead of asking Darian to look at the data, I ask Victor. I can't quite put my finger on it. Since Darian is surely up to something, I feel like I can trust Victor a little more. Even though he too thinks I'm a romance writer with my head in the clouds.

The 'soft' sciences, my ass. I'm corroborating the *actual history of this city* and that's what they'd call me.

I don't know, maybe they're right.

October 1

I am curious about K., but there is also the fear of insulting a dangerous man by impugning his identity in some way, which every woman perceives with a sense keener than any other. V. also has this sense, I feel certain, though I can't imagine why. Where did I get that idea? Maybe I am simply incapable of seeing him clearly.

But K., I see clearly. He's educated, affable, a little older than me; he's clearly losing weight now that he's joined our neighbourhood, I mean, so fast it's almost visible; even his thick hairline recedes as swiftly as a grassfire chomping great swathes out of a meadow. By joining with us, he has left behind some secret manner of feeding himself, and now he eats like we do. He could leave, I think ferociously, watching him and V. as we cross the city, as agile as rats. He could leave us.

But he won't.

Now, why is that?

It used to not be a relevant question; people just sort of clustered up, huddled together. Babes in a storm. But now, with the entire city at our disposal, you can go anywhere, and people do; you can survive alone, and people do. He's obviously been doing well. So why leave them, and come to us?

The sinister sparkle of that golden beard, like candyfloss!

He joins us now, me and V. and occasionally the taciturn P., as we search for the missing. I would not have asked him, but we have so few people, and we are looking for people who are so few. Whole blocks, whole neighbourhoods, have no human life within them whatsoever, only the statues of our conquerors, their faces grossly smug, as if they are proud of having driven everyone out of the area. We get nothing good, nothing useful, from these people. In movies, I think angrily sometimes as we plod up and down the streets, we would have found an informant by now. But maybe (I think, and I think V. does too) we are carrying one with us.

We've moved flats, quietly and without comment. Now we are in some airy, Art Deco monstrosity, room after room of soothing curves, no angles, plush rugs, and (importantly) intact doors. We boarded up the windows that first afternoon. Remember a world where we liked to have large panes of glass at ground level? Shudder to remember. We are far, far from our old neighbourhood, and even though I returned and gave everyone our new address, I fret about my lost neighbours, my lost people. I feel very far away from them, not a half-hour walk. (If only we could use bicycles! But that was a useful lesson to learn, too.)

At night, we climb to the roof and survey the darkened city with binoculars. V. often bores of this and turns his on the sky, which of course is terrible with binoculars and makes him motion sick.

Look, he said last night, startled, scrambling to his feet, and I rushed to his side, but saw nothing where he pointed.

You're not being pulled again, are you, I complained.

No! I just... I think I saw the ISS pass, he said, and his face crumpled in the moonlight, all exaggerated pain in silver and black. I took his flashlight from him quickly before he collapsed to the roof and sat motionless, head in hands.

Oh my God, I said. Oh, God.

Silence fell as we stared up at the sky again, in vain; clouds had begun to gather, softly covering the stars, a chunk of bright moon, till everything was snowed under its diffuse powdery light.

I never thought of that, I never looked up. But the astronauts up there, had they gotten a visit from Them as well? Was the whole space station dead, mad, vomiting strange languages? A slow starvation, or a swift death by thirst?

I'm so sorry, I wanted to tell them, that no one will come get you. I'm so sorry. We do remember you.

Far below us, snorting and pacing, the statues prowled the streets. Their feet were like nails on chalkboard. Come up here and say that, I wanted to yell.

I wish we had proper siege equipment for this siege, V. muttered. Pour a big cauldron of boiling oil on them.

Drop a rock on them, K. said.

Yes, I said. Like in the books.

How would I catch Darian in the act?

I'm not even going to talk to the others. Winnie would try to talk me out of it (and succeed). Victor would stay neutral. But I am adamant, quietly, that the story that Eva is telling is worth sharing with the world, and its veracity can only be questioned by reasonable persons. That's all. That's all I want to say. That's all I want to prove. And Darian, I am sure, just as adamantly, does not want me to prove that.

What a ridiculous thought. We're all focusing on our own research here.

Victor says the deer appear quite normal. "Even their droppings," he says.

"I'm not helping you collect deer shit, Victor."

And now I find I'm missing files. What the hell? I've talked to the other three and they say nothing's out of the ordinary at their stations. "Mice," Victor said uncertainly. "Check the back for droppings. Or ants."

I tried to meet Darian's eye, but he held his gaze steadily till I dropped mine. "You probably just mis-filed them," he said brusquely. "It happens."

I don't want him to talk down to me, I want him to

admit that he's been tampering with my research. There isn't much missing—just photos and a scan of the one badge that I found in the dirt by the hospital, and the inscription on the back, because it occurred to me that most of the badges I've read about don't have an inscription. It's not in any of the Cyrillic languages; I have the scanner trying to parse what it says. So there's still *some* files. But not the high-quality original. I'm ticked off.

What I want, really, is to catch him in the act. But what act? He's rarely even near the pod during the day, and at night we're all there.

Maybe I'm just being paranoid.

After all, he'd say, you don't have any evidence. And if he looked (gulp) he'd find, probably, traces that I've been in his files, too. But he wouldn't give them to me if I asked. And I didn't delete anything.

I would not want to tell V. or Eva, by the way, that the ISS crashed about five years after the end of the Setback. No survivors, of course, but no way of determining whether there were remains on board either. Only scraps were recovered from the ocean. Maybe they were spared, there. Maybe they weren't.

October 3

The bloody agents go around stealing guns, emptying the city. Cleansing the city of ammunition till we are toothless. Oh, how I hate Them for that, <u>hate</u> Them. We are reduced to cavemen, to fighting with fists and nails and teeth and clubs, as if we had not even invented the spear. What are They so afraid of? And They are cracking down even more on gatherings; the number grows smaller and smaller, till we can meet and speak only in our handfuls. Any speck of light, any wisp of smoke, any betrayal of habitation is enough for Them to rush in and search.

The old women say this is like the old days, and I nod, because I too read the history books, and they tell me: No, no Eva. This is not like the books. This is what the books cannot truly tell you. The invasion of privacy, the rush of the warm air into the icy night.

They are looking for rebellion and sedition, and in other places, other times, the mere act of looking used to create it; but it cannot do so here. They stamp it out, and then if even the wind stirs the remains, They stamp again. You've seen what They did to that first revolution, and I think, yes, I did see, I wish I could forget. We're no good at this revolution thing now, I think. Ours was erased, actually obliterated, so that not even teeth remained.

What they needed was a cadre of old women, which are still in no short supply in this place; in fact after M. disappeared I began to notice how some people simply soldiered on. The world of old women had not ended; only ours had. They had lived under one dictator and then another and another, and when the system collapsed and strangers came to their houses to tell them they were free, their answers were "Hah!" Universal disdain. Now, strangers come to their houses to ask them if they would like a few cans of sardines, and their answer is "Hah!"

I think of the first days, eating next to that old woman,

how she had honed her own knife to a razor's edge and taken apart someone's leg as smoothly and quickly as if she'd been doing it all her life, like deboning a chicken, so that for a moment we others around the fire glanced at one another: <u>Had</u> she been doing it all her life? Good Lord, the police never find most serial killers, do they.

But she had something we didn't: transferable skills. The rest of us lost ours in the unconquered years.

The city shifts, rumbles at night. We leap out of sleep in fits and starts, whimpering like babies startled awake. Sometimes, when we do so, K. is not there. I tell myself: It means nothing. It's better than thinking that it means everything. That it's proof of something. I haven't told the others; I'm not sure they've noticed.

A. tells me, nervously, that he's heard that They've taken one of the old war bunkers near the river as Their new headquarters. That you can see Them sometimes, shapeless and tall as mountains, flickering in and out of it, leaving behind Their stench and the soil writhing with Their leavings. The bunker was some kind of tourist attraction (for the dozen tourists we used to get every summer) but still structurally functional, still solid, still good. Three-foot walls of solid rebar concrete. You'd have to drop a bomb square on it to make a dent. We joke about this city and its flimsy new buildings, but a lot of the older stuff is like that—swoops and blocks of concrete, whole riverbeds of moulded aggregate. You never appreciate the stuff while you're baking in a bus station made of it, and yet it never rots, warps, weeps like wood; it doesn't flake or chip like brick; a thrown stone won't shatter it like glass, but bounce back. We bitch about it, journalists come here and photograph it to mock in coffee-table books, but dammit, it's useful. You can tell from all the hits this city's taken. What falls. What stands.

If <u>you</u> were gathering children from a dead city's dead parents, would you put them behind concrete? Or something else?

October 8

Our people never threw out much, we hoarded and buried for later, proud of our full pantries, we knew the word 'cache' and laughed when the magpies and squirrels did it. Is that what They are doing with the children? Are They storing them for... for something I cannot think of? Or are They waiting till they grow up and become suitable for use as agents?

The not knowing hurts me, a long unending throb. It is still all I can think of and I am making myself sick with it.

One good thing today: V. brought food for dinner at the old flat, not a full community dinner, though there would have been enough: just me, P., K., A., B., and T1 and T2, whom I have noticed are absolutely impossible to kill, and also impossible to get behind; we have a game now, which I am sure they participate in as fully as V. and I, where we try to get behind them, but they always have their backs to a wall.

The food, anyway. A plateful of bleeding, dark red meat. P. and I looked at each other. We looked at K., who showed no surprise. T1 and T2 snickered.

Oh, come on, said T2, and dug her skinny elbow into

V.'s side. I thought we agreed we would stop doing that.

It's not what you think! V. said.

Yes, it's one thing to eat the already dead, said T1 serenely, and another to get, you know. Fresh provisions. Shame on you, young man.

It's not that! V. huffed. It's venison!

We all laughed. And I really mean that. Laughed and laughed as if he had told one of those long obscene jokes. And cooked the meat on spits in the fireplace like cavemen, and burned our fingers while we gorged ourselves, absolutely gorged, till our stomachs were distended. With nothing on it, not even salt, it tasted like... the meal you might be given in Heaven, you swoop in on your cloud and they hand you your wings and a plate of steak and potatoes, charred and rare like this, it tasted like pepper and rosemary, brown butter, fried garlic, it tasted like dreams. When the only true seasoning, looked at in the cruel light of daylight, was cooked blood from a fresh corpse.

(Update later: it _was_ a deer! V. stubbornly showed me the hooves and the startled head, still dripping. They wandered into the park, he said. Three of them. A tree snatched at them and they bolted right into me, and I stabbed one of them. Then I had to chase it down. Thought it would taste gamey. I laughed, As if any of us would notice whether it did, you ridiculous creature. He had a smear of blood under his eye. Funny, I said, pointing at it, it suits you, Nimrod the noble hunter, and he said, Then I'll keep it there. We agreed not to eat the brain, even though it was probably full of valuable minerals and vitamins and suchlike. Mad Deer Disease, I said.)

* * *

"There should be a cache or an armoury somewhere in the city," I tell him. "The agents were confiscating weapons, but I bet they weren't destroying them."

"Could be," Darian says.

"Did... have you found anything like that?"

"Nope."

I almost say, pleadingly, 'Are you sure?' and then I realize that that's what he wants me to do: plead. For his help. He's a bully, but is he anything more than that? I need to find out.

The city shifts gently, rumbles at night, just as Eva said. We're used to earthquakes back home, but here they seem more unsettling. And it doesn't help with the nightmares, either. There are new cracks forming in the buildings from all the seismic activity. Darian's instruments can tell the difference between these and the ones formed by bombs, statues, looters, and time, which I admit seems a bit like magic to me, which I guess makes him a wizard. But I'd never give him the satisfaction of admitting it.

The pull, the pull from the stars. What does that *mean*?

God, maybe I really should be doing qual instead of quant. Maybe then I would have some answers.

October 11

K. told us he's "got a lead."

Oh, really, said V.

The old seminary on the south side of the city, he said. Do you know it?

I knew it; V. did not, clearly, but as he had been born and raised here I could see that he would be damned if he admitted it. It had been abandoned after the war, when the priests were rounded up and marched off, and then it had become some government administration building for a while, and then it was declared structurally unsound in the 'nineties and closed off. The city was supposed to rebuild it or prop it up or something, but there always seemed to be something else to do with the money. A practical, modestly adorned concrete building of three or four storeys, sagging dangerously in the middle.

I met K's eyes and drew myself up. Who told you this? I said. What did they see?

An old woman I met, he said. Near the riverfront. She was doing laundry, and fell in, and I pulled her away from those tentacle-things that grow up between the rushes, and we talked. I didn't tell her I was looking for missing children.

No? I said.

He said, No. I told her I was looking for places the sentinels and the statues came in and out of a lot. All day. All night. And she said, oh, like an anthill, the opening of an anthill. The old seminary.

Let's go then, I said. Let's look.

V. said, No, it's too close to night. We'll have to go tomorrow. All of us. Together.

Of course, said K.

Under some pretext, he wandered off, humming to himself; V. and I narrowed our eyes at him as he left.

He's got a nice voice, said V. after a minute. You'd believe someone who told you things with a voice like that.

Oh, you noticed that too, I said. I noticed that he knows this city, but he doesn't love it.

No? said V.

I waved an arm at the plaza around us, the thick old buildings tottering but still proud, the church with its breathlessly bent steeple, the bell hanging over the edge like a perched bird, the whole square barely recognizable now, as if it fell from a great height. The gray concrete, the colour of the gray sky, loomed over us like the clouds, angular, the edges soft with impact, chunks littering the ground snowlike at the base of every foundation. You don't have to love a place just because you've lived here a long time, I said. I mean, look at you. You've lived here less time than me.

How do you know that? he said.

I'm much older than you, I said patiently.

Not much, he said. I bet.

How much do you bet?

A billion American dollars, he said blithely. No, don't give me that look; I know where I can lay my hands on it. I could be the richest man in the country in half an hour. The continent.

It's true, I said.

Money doesn't mean much now. It didn't even mean much when we had the proper markets still going. It was just food for food.

And I was thinking of Chornobyl, hundreds of kilometers away but in a sense very near, near enough to touch, as if its breath were on the back of my neck; They were there too, I knew. It was even a site of curiosity for Them if not gladness, it was a place They congregated, a place whose poison They might even enjoy; I felt certain, somehow, stabbingly sure, that they had broken the Sarcophagus, taken the Elephant's Foot into the obscenities of Their mouths. I wondered what V. knew about it. Just what they taught in the history books. But he had been born years after that happened, and I had been born before. It was different.

It's not different, he said, months before when I brought it up. Both people born before and after it happened carry the mark in their bones. Because the fallout got everywhere. It's like a signature. No, a tattoo.

No, that's not true, I said. It was only for people who were born before.

No, it's everyone, he insisted. The only difference is degree.

I'm doubtful that that can be true, but what do I know about bones? At any rate, I can't go to the library and take out a book about it, not right now. Maybe in the winter, if we're still alive. Isn't it funny that that was virtually the only thing the world knew about us, when they thought of us at all, and it took the Invasion for the entire world to start thinking about the same thing all at once. Solidarity at last, I thought, and I laughed drily by myself in the dark.

October 15

Happy birthday to me! If I've been reckoning the days right, I suppose. I think I am the only person in the city who still adheres to some kind of calendar and it's probably not even accurate by this point.

We set off across the city this morning, just as we said, to investigate the seminary. Everything soft, silent, waiting. As if holding its breath. I scanned the ground as we walked, hoping to find... what? I don't know. Something obvious and clear that no one could miss. A dropped shoe smaller than my palm. A superhero sticker.

And ahead of us—a shock, an expected shock, our stomachs telling us first that the ground was moving, and only then seeing it erupt, spitting cobbles into the houses near us, a humped thing slavering and gnashing at us, its tongue covered in our good black soil. I say this now, as if I had stood and coolly analyzed its appearance, but in fact we spun and ran so fast that we got no more than a glimpse. It was big, like a bull, but it was fast once it dug itself out of the street, and the street itself shivered under our running feet, and we fell to hands and knees and kept going.

Of course it was a trap. When we had staggered and sprinted and crawled about fifteen blocks the thing ceased its pursuit, and we had no strength except to crawl into a doorway and count our fingers and toes and teeth. You did this, I almost said to K. You brought us into this. And yourself, to make it look credible. But we were all so shattered and ragged that I resolved to do it in private, and then did not.

V. said, That's a good sign. They wouldn't have put that thing there if They had nothing to protect.

K. said nothing.

We met tonight, briefly, to discuss the trap, and the possibility of getting the children, if they are alive. I want people to be... well. No. Let us be clear. I want to coerce everyone into helping me. I don't care if they do it out of guilt. But I myself will feel guilty if I guilt them into helping us.

P. is passionate, but has no plan. She stood on the coffee table in her ripped leggings and said, Listen. I was a student at the university. I was on campus on Invasion Day. My parents, my sisters, my brother, they are dead far from here—two thousand kilometers from here. This isn't my city, this isn't even my country. I will never go home again. But I'm willing to stay and fight because we cannot break the chain of what links the past to the future. If we die, who will tell the stories of those who survived the old conquerors?

And T1 said: Thousands of years of conquerors. Not just these, nor the last ones, nor the ones before that.

Silence fell while we thought of how we have all been overrun, how this land has always been under someone's thumb, and I still wonder where P. is from and how many times her country was overrun. I cannot place her accent. At any rate we all know that the last time no one saw fit to invade anyone else's land, we still, probably, swung from the trees. What people want, always, is to conquer. To take what belongs to the seemingly weak or the outnumbered or the outgunned... to take from the other. If you erase an entire generation and replace it with your own, the chain breaks, both ends swing free.

She came here to learn about the past, to carry it into the future. She loves that chain. She does not want it to break.

Me, I don't know how I feel about it. But I suppose I will continue keeping this diary as long as I can. Hearing her, last night, I wondered who picked sides, if they had been undecided before; I wondered if it felt like it had when I did, abruptly, with a sensation like swooning or falling into an unfamiliar darkness.

It is we who must forge the links of that chain to get the children out. No one else will.

WAKING IN HYSTERIA, screaming, slapping at the light panels, no light, darkness, bolting into the night, crashing into something heavy, a statue, no, something else, a sentinel!

It is Darian, startled, his hands in front of his face for a moment to protect it from my feeble half-asleep slapping; at last he takes my wrists in his hands, warm and damp, and stares at me as if I were the last thing anyone had expected to see on the planet. "Emerson?"

I'm sputtering, I cannot speak. At last I explain that there was something in my room, something in there with me, something that touched me, that slid in through the angle between wall and ceiling from another place, and fell onto my cot, and touched me—

He's staring at me, honestly baffled. "A rat," he offers a moment later, and lets me go, and even puts his hands on my shoulders for a second, surprising us both. "One of Winnie's rats, maybe?"

"No! It wasn't a rat. Or maybe, I don't know."

I'm shivering in my thin night clothes, not pajamas but a t-shirt and cargo pants, not dissimilar but lighter than the stuff I wear during the day ("Always," Dr. Aaron told us, "wear something you can run in"), and he starts to steer me back towards the pod.

I resist for a second, dig my socked feet into the sharply rubbled ground. Let the sun come up, I want to beg him. But then I go limp, and we walk back to the pod, and it's warm inside, and there is nothing, of course, in my room; we check every corner, awkwardly weaving around each other, his big body and my small one far too much for the little space. It is spotless, no footprints, no spoor, no fur.

"Nightmare," I say, as we eat breakfast, when Winnie asks me what all the noise was about.

"Oh, I've been getting those here," she says. "I suppose it's the—you know." She waves her spoon around at the dead city. "Full immersion in the most gruesome place I've ever been in my life."

"Yeah."

Chernobyl, Eva said. I jump to see the word on the screen. Yes. It did split open, during the Invasion or the Setback or shortly after, and has only recently been brought back under control, somewhat, with a nanofilament shell around it like a huge honeycomb. The grumpy stalwarts still living nearby, eating their irradiated berries and mushrooms, had all vanished, of course, like virtually everyone else. No bodies. No one goes there to study now. Maybe in a hundred years or so. When we are all dead, and have passed our torches to yet another generation of eager students.

Was it a rat I saw? I'm sure I saw *something*.

This idea Eva had, that They were gods or something, I can't get behind that, but I can't shake it either. They had the trappings of gods, maybe They had fooled other worlds. But no hint of real divinity, except for power.

Gods have a system.

October 20

Tried to return to the seminary, harried and trapped by sentinels. But, predicting it, V. and I had armed ourselves like road warriors, and somewhat to our surprise, killed (I think?) one of the statues.

The body, seemingly solid brass, vanished into a pool of bubbling sludge (ask around: has anyone seen that?) but the head that we so inefficiently and with such effort cut off with the shovel remained startlingly, even alarmingly intact. One eye open, one eye shut, instantly glazed as if it had been sprayed with paint.

We studied it for a while, panting, arms over our mouths and noses from the smell of its... well. You can't say blood. It was too runny, and black and blue, and glittering, and flowed briefly over the ground, wilting the grass as it went. I watched it flow over a discarded screw, and sputter and fizz into transparency for a moment.

We should keep it as a trophy, I said.

Definitely not, V. said. I don't want that anywhere near where I'm sleeping.

That's a good point, I said, but reluctantly; you know you can kill the sentinels, and you know you can sort of pause the statues, but it's still academic until you are actually standing over one, watching your shovel melt away from the wooden handle.

There, he said. That's a proper act of war, anyway.

Yes, I said. We should get to paint one on the side of our tank.

Or plane.

Yes.

But we'd need a tank or a plane.

There's a lot of tanks, I said thoughtfully, in that park on the other side of town.

Maybe, he said, we should just draw one on our arms instead.

I wish we'd had a guillotine, I said. That took forever.

We kept looking at the head, and then I began to feel nauseated, and faint, and we staggered away to get some fresher air. But I felt good. Hopeful, even. Not, I mean, that it's good to kill—I don't mean that. But that it's good to kill if what you're killing wants to kill you all the time and has killed just about, but not quite, everyone you loved.

In the playground near our new flat, we sat on the swings and ate ornamental crabapples, wincing at the splendid tartness. I said, We would fight if we could, but we can't. We would surrender if we could, but we can't. What do you suppose that's doing to people's minds?

V. shrugged. Well. It's not like we had some... pre-existing understanding that... you know. That this dimension belonged to us.

No pact of non-aggression or whatever.

No. We haven't been betrayed. I just keep wondering... why us? Why here? When They could be anywhere?

Maybe They have a different map of the world than we do, I said hopelessly. Maybe there's a note on certain cities saying MONSTERS WELCOME HERE.

He said, We keep setting off Their traps. How can we get to the seminary?

I said, We need more people.

November 1

I have to write this down.

K. said, idly, while we were digging the summer potatoes, You know, negotiation with Them may not be possible, but we don't know what other places are doing.

I was only half-paying attention, I was sweaty, thirsty. I said, What does that mean?

He said, How do you think we've all survived in the past? Not knuckling under, that's not what I mean. Not making offerings. Just... going along with things. Being compliant.

I filled one more bucket, I think, before I straightened up and looked at him. The wind picked up and his hair gleamed for a second in the sunlight, like the glossy grass around us. I didn't glare, I didn't frown, I didn't yell or rant or wave my trowel. Only inside came a shrill, frightened yowl, drowning out all reason. I took a few deep breaths.

I said, Appeasement, you mean.

No! What an awful, ugly word. And the time for that is past, anyway. I mean, working together. Cooperation. At least for a little while.

Ah, I said.

He said, To let humanity recoup, give us a little breathing room without being so... so constantly persecuted. For God's sake, it's not capitulation. It's common sense. You know They are mostly cracking down on people who offend Them in some way. I don't know. I am just thinking aloud here.

He was, too. And I wondered whose benefit that was for, who was listening aside from us. The grass around us rustled, but it was windy, the wind fluting through the broken glass dome, I remember that. The weeds and wildflowers looked all right, only a few twisted, with translucent, milky panes in their stems or petals, faceted like the eyes of insects. Their rich smell was all around us. I thought: If you are very small and the bees cannot see you, they will have to find you some other way; you cannot stay a secret if it is not your life's purpose to be a secret. But you can if there are no bees.

His speech didn't sound rehearsed. Of course, if I were a spy, I would rehearse it till it didn't.

I said, mildly, Well, we've had thousands of years of people 'cracking down' on us for doing things like being located inconveniently. Or objecting to the seizing of our rail line. Or our people. Or fighting back. Or eating. Or breathing. I mean, they say Kyiv changed hands fourteen times in eighteen months, back in the day.

He watched me in silence, leaning on his hoe. Who was listening? Who was there?

I said, Look, we know the routine; it's been a thousand years. Some asshole with a moustache barges in, he barely has time to turn around, you get some other asshole with a moustache. And they've all been putting up statues of themselves that we have to pull down and re-cast later. The least you can say about our newest conquerors is that the things growing on their faces cannot be positively identified as hair.

He laughed; I laughed. Separately, one after the other. Inside, I felt something roiling, a witch's cauldron of black iron filled to the brim with things struggling to break the surface, thick bubbles popping; I felt sick, I felt <u>certain</u>.

But as the afternoon passed the feeling faded and now I am left, at the end of the day, with K. and V. sleeping in the living room and me thinking: Did I remember right, did I remember the conversation right? Maybe that's not what he said. Maybe I'm exaggerating.

More than usual tonight I feel that I am being watched, in this windowless room.

APPEASEMENT, OF COURSE—the policy with which I've lived most of my short and academically-focused life—never worked; I suppose Eva wondered whether it had, anywhere. The truth was it never did, but that didn't stop places from trying it. Compliance, as she notes, wasn't the goal of the Invaders; but it was clear that people were disappearing, even their corpses were disappearing, and so there were numerous people who thought, "Well, we have one currency left," and offered up their survivors as payment. But they almost all died right along with their friends. The few witnesses scrambled away with a combination of luck and the carelessness of the un-appeased, already knowing that their narratives would be hard to believe by the scholars of the future.

It wasn't that we believed it or disbelieved it, really; it was that we ate it up too quickly to be objective. Pain is interesting, I was told when I started my studies. People don't want to read about happiness. They want to read about pain. That's what'll get you published.

I search for the seminary, but I suppose it's been destroyed, crumbled over the years. Maybe she will give me another clue. Even though now I'm afraid of what I might find there.

November 10

How did the fight start? I said, I'll go alone. Maybe we're setting off the traps because we go in a group.

No, I'll come with you, he said. You don't need to prove how brave you are.

I opened my mouth and shut it, stunned. No, I am a coward, I wanted to tell him. Valentin! Don't you know that? Don't you know me by now?

Till the world ended I thought I was average, I thought I had an average level of... everything. Two children, one husband, just enough school, just enough intelligence, just enough height and boobs and heft and courage. I took home a pay packet that, combined with M.'s, precisely let us keep house, go on vacation once a year, and buy the latest shiny flat phones to annoy each other with.

But when the day came, when the day came... there we were, the average four of us utterly unwarned for the tearing open of air and light. Terrified, we thought to flee to the countryside, but we let our terror paralyze us a little too long, and then we had to stay. And then the boys drafted into the defense... I remember embracing N., already so skinny, a growing boy forced by semistarvation to stop growing, his familiar body under my hands like a pillowcase full of twigs.

They will go fight in the countryside outside the walls, we thought. We already knew that was where Their reach did not often go, since everyone is so spread out—our country has a big side. We thought the boys would be safer out there, not subject to the raids, the vanishings, the interrogations, the bombs, the ugly new statues that walked at night and left only greasy patches of blood and fat by dawn. Then we thought: if we stay in the city, the boys will find us again. Out there, only They will find us.

And we stayed, drawing fire. I think now of the birds that feign a broken wing to lure predators away from the nest and I wonder which of us, in city or country, might be that bird. I don't even know if they are still alive. The last message I got was over a year ago, when people could still sneak in and out of the city to a limited extent.

I worry that the boys said something that will tip Them off, or Their agents, that they have found a way to draw bulls-eyes on their backs. I worry that they will try to reach me. I worry that they won't. I worry that there is a word for children without parents, but none for a parent who has lost both her children.

Well. Put that way, what have I, cowardly lion, to lose? More than V. Less than the others. I don't know.

And yet, I keep thinking of that darkness, it must be dark in there, They would not keep the children in a place with light; in fact, I don't even think They see light at all.

I think: They come from a place where the light is not like this. Or doesn't exist. They don't care.

The children in the darkness, I can't bear it. I think of N. and I. and I think... the light on their faces that last day, their light, terrified, laughing faces as they left me, the blue of their eyes just like M's. At least they left together. Oh, God!

We have to go.

We cannot stay.

November 16

Confirmed. Really, we needed more bodies, more eyes, but we got there in the end, by pitiful subterfuge that would not have fooled a doddering mall security guard. I don't know why we didn't think of it before. We just... set roughly an entire street on fire, and let the sentinels come out, screaming in surprise, and in the confusion we ran the other way.

The old seminary has its own cemetery, crawling with fist-sized monsters, their bodies bright and insulting on the ancient stones. I bared my teeth looking at it, I felt hatred crawl over my own body, I wanted to rush in there and sweep them away, slap them, like roaches or centipedes. They are ruining the inscriptions. But anyway: the grass there impossibly, sinisterly green, still, despite the coming winter, just as V. said.

I put P. on watch. I don't know how I feel about her, but I trust her instincts; she's the wariest person I've ever met, she has been watching for enemies since long before the Invasion. V. and I crept down, listening, trying locked doors, tapping on the stone and brick. Expecting, still, to find nothing. Streets away, we heard the roar of the fire, and things thinly screaming; I had to close my eyes and press my entire face to the building before I heard anything.

When the voice emerged from the hole, V. cried aloud; I almost did too. We stooped, pressed our ears to the grille. We could pry this off, he whispered. I told him to shut up.

A thin voice from the stinking darkness. The hole, covered with a wire grille on our side, thick, screwed into the cement.

Hello? Is that... who are you?

I told the child our names. The things, I said. The monsters, the... Them. They've been stealing you, taking you down here?

Yes. We've been here for... I don't know. Maybe a year? It's gotten cold twice. I'm Olga, the child said. There are twenty-seven of us. It's my job to keep count because I'm the oldest.

V. and I both looked down there, but we couldn't see anything; I assumed that the grille was set up too high, and they had nothing to stand on. Behind us, a faint, warbling chirp from P., on the roof of the adjacent building. A long, cold wind. Leaves spattering us from the un-turned trees. All our greatest fears come true, and only one hope: that the children were alive.

Do you know why They took you? I asked.

No, said the child. They never said.

I daresay They wouldn't, I said.

We used to call out of the hole, she said, but then we heard... we heard people coming to help us, and the... monsters... always...

It's all right, I said hastily. Don't feel bad.

She said, So we stopped.

Are They hurting you? Are They... experimenting on you? I said. Behind me, V. said: Eva. Shut up, I told him.

Olga said, No. But there isn't much to eat. And sometimes people come by and they... take us out. Usually the young ones. And they don't come back.

After a judicious pause she added, They haven't taken me yet, of course, because I'm almost eleven.

I said, Sit tight. We're coming to get you out. Soon. We'll come back. We'll come back.

No reply. I suppose she doesn't believe us. I wouldn't either. And what if it's... I can't help but think. What if I don't believe *her*? What if it's a monster or something, imitating her voice? Are They capable of something like that? What if it's a trap, meant to lure in the very, very last few survivors?

I can't believe, though, that They would think of that.

The doors are chained shut, the windows boarded. Next time, V. said as we ran back to the flat, we'll bring some bolt-cutters and get in there, and... But I wasn't listening.

I am already planning. We can't, I think, go in through the inside. Too many hallways and doors, good for an ambush. We'd be ripped to bits. But from the outside, where no one expects it...

I don't think They would play a trick like that, V. said when I brought up my theory about the voices. But I can believe that Their agents would. That's an old trick, a wartime trick. They lure you with something. Warehouses full of food. Ammo dumps. Hostages, POWs. Wives. Children. And then, when enough soldiers fall for the lure...

That's true, I said. And we fell silent.

There's ages of majority, I thought, and before that, we as adults are assumed to be the custodians of the young. We make decisions for them. We pick them up, we put them down. We drive them around. We tell them: You will go to such-and-such a school, you will study such-and-such an instrument. Oh, there may be some input; but we don't allow them to be decision-makers, we don't allow active participation in their lives. Maybe other parents did, I don't know. But there's no five year-olds I would trust to make a good decision about their future, because they'd just run right into the street.

And yet, I did not ask these children: Do you want to come out? Into the world? It will not be the world you remember.

Of course, they've been kidnapped by transdimensional monsters. If anyone says 'No' I suppose it'll just be Stockholm Syndrome.

Still, though.

November 17

We have a plan, not a good one, and depending equally on luck that we cannot count on, science we do not know, and risks of which we are blithely and necessarily ignorant. Truly, it is the kind of plan you picture people coming up with in the old days, when their brains were mush from hunger and propaganda, when everything seemed like a good idea.

Back in the old neighbourhood, we four, our strange

little family, gathered at A.'s place, and he called in the others as surreptitiously as he could over the space of a few hours. I made a speech. V. made a speech. P. curled up on the sagging sofa and chewed on her knuckles till they bled. You're just a child yourself, I wanted to tell her, but of course, if she was at the university, she was in every respect not. But I keep comparing her to me and thinking: Look at you, I have a pair of shoes older than you.

I think I do, too. Or did.

The others fell silent after we spoke; B. rocked back and forth, and watched me, his mouth opening and closing as if he was going to speak. An inconclusive meeting. We made no new recruits. Disheartening: and we have no means to do what we plan anyway. Hell, by the time we figure something out, all the kids might be gone. But if we don't go back soon, they'll lose hope.

The time has come to pray, but I find myself speaking into a humming void: not the proud and obnoxious atheism of my twenties, not the uncertain agnosticism of my childhood, but just... calling a line, and hearing it ring and ring and ring, no one picking up. Pick up, I beg, and I clasp my hands now at night. Let me feel as if there's something there.

Perhaps They have usurped God too, shoved Their way into where He lives, I don't know. If there are any strange angles up there, They will find them; They always do. I find myself childishly, exhaustedly glad our new flat is all curves and circles.

Instead of praying for help or comfort I find myself mumbling at night to the children who cannot hear me.

Here, children, I will say when we get them out. We have saved you; we have delivered you into this world that some of you may remember, and some of you may well not.

Here, you must know the good guys from the bad guys.

The bad guys no longer label themselves with sharp black uniforms or mangled crosses, nor do they bear our flag, or the badge of our city; they are like and unlike the simple images in your schoolbooks. Do you remember those?

I make these speeches to myself in here only. I would never say such things to children.

And yet: Look, children, we have rescued you. You owe us nothing, not even your gratitude; and we owe you everything, merely for staying alive. But I want you to look carefully at this world.

Here are the bad guys. Are you paying attention?

Hunger. Thirst. Illness. Injury.

Rain. Snow. Dust.

Sickness. Loneliness. Despair. Mistrust.

Agents. Looters. Rats.

The statues of the conquerors.

The trees which seek to seize and skin you.

The small monsters which seek to harry and eat you.

The Them, who have come from far away, and a different time, to drag you into the darkness. But Them you already know.

Did They speak to you, in the darkness? What did They tell you? Did They admit that They were the enemy? It should have been clear to you that They were, but you are all very young. Well, never fear. We have gotten you out.

I choke on: And I will be your mother now.

I'm a mother already. I'm a mother of two. That is part of me, part of who I am. But where are they now? They're fighting and they were too young to fight, I—

I weep now, writing these words. We will never get them out, will we? And then even if we survive, it will be for nothing. Nothing, absolutely nothing.

I rehearse the plan in my head, I stare at the lines on my left palm, cramped around this pen, but conveniently, even mystically, aligned with the map I have in my head. Here, this bubble on my lifeline is the old seminary; and here is the river, its ice cracking under the weight of a sparrow; and here are the train tracks; and here is the lake; and here, at my wrist, where the blood beats thickly in the green veins, is freedom.

Oh, we can't do this. What were we thinking?

What will we do?

November 18

B. is dead. Note how I don't say 'missing.' Confirmed. Added to the tally at the back of the book.

No burial place.

And he couldn't even—I hate to say it. He couldn't even hang himself? Neatly, quietly? Or shoot himself? We would not have begrudged him the bullet. There's lots of ammunition left if you know where to look in the city, and there must still be handguns around here and there.

No, I'm sorry to say, he concocted some kind of homemade device and blew up not merely himself but his entire building.

We had returned early from the harvest, rather than right at sundown. A good thing, too. We were far too close. If we had been closer he would have taken us with him, I think. But we all looked up at once, and saw him standing in the window, waving at us. It did not occur to me to run. I just looked up. I waved, even, I think. I can't remember.

He was on the top floor, the fourth floor. So the building collapsed slowly and drunkenly, swaying, weakened, and then down, the third floor, then down again, the second. Really it was much less dramatic than I think he intended for it to be. And less lethal. We avoided the worst of the shrapnel, half a block away, but there was so much dust, a mushroom cloud of it, like a nuke. White, white concrete dust. It wasn't even as loud as I thought it would be.

We all stood there for a second, mouths open.

And then in the wake of the explosion, a dreamy moment, the kind you dream of as a teenager; V. overwhelmed, half-flattened with shock, lowering his head to my shoulder, placing his arm around my waist. I could have turned by the minutest amount, gone up on my tiptoes, and kissed him square on the mouth. Instead I raised my numb and trembling hand to his pillowy curls, and we stood there a moment, letting warmth bloom between us. And I too let hope bloom: That he feels the same way as I do, that he was seeking something more than comfort and safety in the arms of a friend. My nose was bleeding and ran through his hair, I accidentally anointed the dusty nape of his neck. The droplets spelled out, I thought, words of devotion. I felt ill, and giddily happy, and anticipatory, as if a treat I had been long-promised had suddenly arrived.

And then P. came up behind us both and nuzzled into my shoulder and his, and I thought as I put my arm around her, with a sudden daggerlike sickness deep in my gut: No. They are children looking for mama's arms.

I'm too old. What was I thinking? I'm forty-five, I'm too old to even think this; they should be with each other.

It only lasted a second, anyway. And then we had to run. The sound had attracted some sentinels, and though we couldn't see them in the dust, I could hear Their shrill cries to each other, the grunts and growls. Ears ringing, faces buzzing, we ran. I set the pace, for once. I think the others were still in shock.

Not just a death, but a death like that. A death we have not seen in well over a year, and right at our feet.

Later, V. and I left P. sleeping in A.'s flat and gingerly returned to the glowing rubble. I felt callous, scheming, a Shakespearean villainess. V. just seemed numb.

If he left a note, V. said, it's probably gone now.

I said nothing. And I grow increasingly convinced that it was an accident.

And also: What did he use? How much material did he leave behind? Was it dynamite? Homemade gelignite? Is there enough to make more bombs?

He did not leave enough of himself to even bless and bury. But he must have left something else.

Thoughtfully, quietly, not talking much, we ate the last dried strawberries of summer from our pockets and roamed around the ruins, looking for instruments of death. Instead, it may be that we found the means of a very ill-advised rescue.

Eyes gleamed in the dusk as we left, clambering down over the still-smouldering scraps. Just a minute, said V. Some of those are people.

There's something wrong with their eyes then, I said. Let's go.

Run, he said.

We ran.

November 20

Tired. It's getting very cold out there, but is it cold enough? A few skiffs of snow, frost every night. We had to rush to get all the cabbages in, but I barely notice the weather except as it relates to the river. My entire mind, my entire life, seems to have shrunk to a pinpoint. As if it were an ocean once, and then it was a lake, and now it is barely a puddle.

We scouted all day today, tiring ourselves in our vigilance. But hit the jackpot (am I using that right?): there's an underground tunnel to the river, leading inadvisably but usefully near the wall of the seminary. (Yes, part of that 'structural instability,' I suspect. The soil must have become waterlogged decades ago.) The tunnel is bricked off, but it resembles the ones still open near the canals.

V. and I tapped on the sides, as if we could tell whether it's filled with water or not, but it doesn't sound like it is. It sounds hollow, promisingly hollow.

Maybe we could use that instead of the train tracks, which are so exposed.

Maybe instead, we could use the train tracks as a decoy.

I don't know. We need to plan. If A. is around later I will go ask him. He was an engineer. Is, I suppose. The Them didn't come here and rip away his certificate, ha ha.

If the river is frozen, we could...

No, I'll ask A. about it. No sense brainstorming in here.

As we left the seminary, V. and I (delightedly, like naughty children) ducked under the snatching branches of the nearby trees, sacrificing the backs of our jackets and a few scraps of skin from wrist and cheek, and dumped bags of salt at their wretched roots, and splashed them with kerosene and set them on fire. What joy, to watch the trunks wither and writhe!

Take that, V. panted as we sprinted away; the cemetery emptied out at our heels in the lowering dusk.

We just gave ourselves away, I said, even though it had been my idea.

They knew already, he said. They knew we were coming.

November 22

K. wavers. What to do about him? I am sure he must hate the status quo as much as any of us, but he also thinks, clearly, if not out loud: Here is the equality we were promised. The weight of the boot presses us all down evenly. And now we must draw attention, shine light upon ourselves, against an invincible enemy? Why not be equal in the dark?

Yes. We must.

Is he an agent?

Listen. When he disappeared two nights ago, slipping out of the flat and silently closing the door, I was up (no mean feat; we spend all day on our feet on scanty rations, and we sleep like the dead at night) and following him. Unsubtly, clumsy in my eagerness not to lose him. He caught me, and took my elbow, gently, and walked me back to the flat. It's not safe, he said. Go back inside. Sleep.

Don't you think I know it's not safe, I said, approximately. Don't you think I know what's out there? Where are you going? Why?

None of your business, he said.

It is my business if you're endangering all of us, I said. What gives you the right? There are three of us to consider. Not just you.

I'm, he said, and hesitated dramatically, his face shifting. Going to see a... a woman.

Oh really, I said.

Yes, he said. Don't follow me. I'll be all right.

I don't care if you're all right or not, I said. Don't ever, ever do it again. Or go find somewhere else to live. Go live with her.

We both know that he is doing nothing of the sort, and I am so angry that he lied to my face as brazenly as that. Like a toddler with his face all jam, denying that he stole it from the fridge. Did he think I would believe him? Did he think I would not be insulted by the lie?

I need to talk to V. If this were another day, another place, we'd run K. through an ordeal. We'd say: Prove that you're not a witch. Now, I watch his hands, I am paranoid. How do They choose their agents? In times of war, or at least times of siege, humans willing to be slaves for a chance to survive must abound; truly, we're either slaves or we're prey. Just prey. Nothing more than that.

How can I find out about K. Maybe he will reveal himself.

Why do I keep asking myself questions that I cannot answer? At least no one will see this book. Unless it is found in the far, far future; but I don't suppose paper will last that long. Maybe I should start thinking of arrangements for it.

That's morbid. I mean, arrangements for its... for its eventual disposition... in the event that...

I mean to say, I must find a final resting place for this book, since I will have no say about the resting place of anything else.

November 23

One last-ditch recruiting speech.

I said: I want to try to make a world that is not like this in some way, <u>any</u> way. Maybe we will kill enough of Them that They will return to Their world. Maybe They will jail us, torture and kill us, no one will know. Maybe They will catch us and make us agents, and our fingers will bleed instead of our faces. But that too will be a different world.

I said, Isn't it worth trying? Are you not already tired of two years under Their reign? They are, you know, the shittiest possible rulers. We should be overthrowing Them just on general principles. But since we cannot, we should at least steal from Them. Aren't you tired?

K. said, Oh God. I am so tired. Yes. Of course I am. But if any agents hear us...

And V's head turned as if it were attached to a string. Of course. I was thinking the same thing. We were among people we know, neighbourhood people. No agents at all. Why was he thinking of them?

If K. is, by some baffling circumstance, not an agent, he is ripe for being turned. Absolutely ripe. Indeed, he would make a good agent, I thought helplessly as he turned away from us. They would not need to break him; he would agree, he would hold out his hand for Their cruel badge, all angles and shivering protrusions. He'd justify it to himself as being for the greater good. No effort would be needed.

He said, The world with Them in it can be survived. What do you think we're doing? People can still have children; who says they can't? I am just saying, you are not being... brave, or noble, or even very clever. You are throwing your lives away like garbage.

No we're not, P. hissed.

We all stared into the fire, and watched our shadows dance on the opposite wall; I waited for horns to sprout on K.'s shadow.

It may be, I think, writhing in agony in my darkest hours, it may be that we cannot get everyone out. It is clear that once we have stolen from Them we cannot stay in the city to await Their punishment. So then we will have to choose. Get only the children out? Or still try for everyone? There is no one I want to leave behind, no one. (Maybe K.) And if it comes down to it (oh, these dark, dark words), I think that no one would volunteer to be left behind.

Please, God, let it not come down to it. Let us all get out.

Maybe the whole world has been overrun with monsters and gods. Maybe we will flee into their very maws. But please, give us the chance to try and to see. Don't let us die here. Don't let us die here.

A. tells me that he can get the train going again. Really, I said. And then paused: <u>Really</u>. Can he? My God, it's like the clouds part, and a single ray of sun shines upon us. If anyone is still wavering, maybe this will push them to one side of the fence or the other. I said, Are you sure?

He shrugged. I was a chemical engineer, he said. Not mechanical. But they did not exactly make it for geniuses to run.

I laughed a little, uncertainly.

I said, The sentinels will all attack the train when it gets running, you know that.

He said, pleased, Yes, of course they will.

I couldn't think of what else to say. This is our last chance to change our minds. We need the river and the lake to be frozen absolutely solid, I just... and now he comes to me, he says this. I had no words. Even now, I have no words.

The dusky whisper in the dark: My name is Olga.

She didn't say: Don't leave us.

I STUDY MY own hand, hoping to see a map like Eva's. Supposedly they're all different, these lines on our palms, but the reality is, everyone's looks virtually the same.

Couldn't she have given me a street name? I exhaust

myself trudging back and forth along the river and the train tracks till I find the train at last, farther along, much farther, than I would have expected to find it. Catching my breath, I photograph it and throw a pilfered drone into the sky for better images, hearing the click in my shoulders. I am dehydrated, I should have taken more water with me. Nothing seems to matter now.

Because there it died, the monstrous locomotive, which must have been ancient even then (our people, Eva said, throw nothing away), still surrounded by the scattered biscuits of coal even now, exploded into a tangle of pipes like tentacles or branches, rusted bright red, covered in claw marks and bubbled with peeled, burned paint.

It's my last moment of happiness. Darian and Winnie find me, and drag me back to the pod for water and cooling packs. "Heat exhaustion," Winnie says. "Couldn't you have stayed in the shade?"

"It's our last day."

"We still have half of tomorrow."

"Our last *full day*," I repeat, and stare up at her, kaleidoscoped from the water beaded on my eyelashes; the cold pack burns my neck, and I fight away from it, trying to sit up on my cot. "Why were you in my files?"

Winnie blinks; Darian glares.

"I wasn't," he says, when it seems clear that Winnie will say nothing.

"You were," I tell him.

"She's delirious."

"Don't lie!" I shout, and sit up, and swat the cold pack against the wall. "Why do you even bother? I set up my station so I could see when other people log in—"

"We *all* log into each other's workstations all the time, Emerson."

"—*and* I added a tracer to my files to see if any of them were being accessed," I snarl, and reach to seize a fistful of his shirt. He bats my hand effortlessly away. "Or changed. Or deleted. And you, not Winnie, not Victor, did all of the above. With the files about the journal I found. The journal that tells the story of the end of this city. The train. The seminary. The tunnel. Even that SOS sign we saw before we came here. Well, joke's on you, pal. Those were fake files you modified. Meant for you to find them. I hid the real ones far down in my private directory."

Winnie does not gasp; but her breath catches. Darian slowly turns purple. Outside, shyly, in the gravel, Victor's shoes scuffle as he waits to come in; I think he probably won't.

"I've got a record," I pant at last. "I've got proof. Isn't that what you're always looking for? Hard evidence? Something you could make into a graph? Because you don't want to think They're gods, do you? That's what bothers you, isn't it?"

"You should get some rest," he says, and tugs Winnie out of my room. As they leave, he says, "She really got some sun out there, didn't she?"

I am furious, I want to chase after him, but I slowly pick up my cold pack again and lie down on the cot, and put it on my chest.

You come back here, I want to scream. I want there to be a fight, a showdown. I want there to be a winner and a loser; I want the others to see that you are wrong and I am right, and that you have been sabotaging my research from the start. I bet if I checked your files I'd find that armoury, wouldn't I. I bet I'd see a yes to all the no's you gave me.

But life isn't like that, and the next day I'm silent as we pack up and board the hover to go home.

November 25

We risked one last visit, scoping, measuring, pacing everything out, and as always, P. shoved a packet of food through the fist-sized hole in the concrete—cooked potatoes, mostly, wrapped in cabbage. I wish we could have done better. Found something sweet for them. But it's either the last of the cold garden, or slop from a goddamned can again, till next spring.

I was terrified for a minute, standing next to P., listening. The room was not merely quiet, it had the silence of death, and not even the reassuring, everyday death of hung meat or slaughtered rabbits, but the recent cessation of intelligent life.

Finally, a whisper: Thank you.

V. had to drag me away from the hole.

The area now is lightly and irregularly guarded. That worries me. The statues scream to each other in the night, I won't say howl—wolves howl, and they are noble animals—and their screams reliably attract others unless you can shut them up. Same with the smaller sentinels, which at least are reasonably killable, like rats, if you can catch them, and if they don't... do that thing where they sort of turn sideways and disappear into a shadow cast by a hair-thin bar of invisible light, you know how it is.

We left our cache against the wall, disguised perfunctorily by a little heap of the ever-present rubble. I kept looking back at it, anxiously, as we slunk out. The sun was going down, sending our shadows in blue and black down the golden street. Did it look too obvious? The trees, the survivors I mean, watched us; who do they talk to, when they are not watching us?

Anyway, the bundle has our crude weapons in it, snowshoes, blankets, plastic sheeting, flares, food, wood. No one knows what we would need to run down the river and cross the lake with the children. But we're going to do our best.

My heart hammers as I write these words. I can see how bad my handwriting's become. Still, even now, any of us could change our mind. But we can't do it unless everyone does it.

We might only have five minutes. One wall goes down as the distraction. Blow the second to open the basement. Drag the kids out, get them on sleds or backs, get the snowshoes on. The train: moving. Then the train: exploding. And us, fleeing.

Writing down the plan strikes me as a mistake now. They would make good use of this if they found it. But maybe They will not find it. Maybe I will carry it with me to freedom. Or it will be found on my body, mutilated on the thick glassy ice of the lake when They catch up with us.

No. Better not to think about it. Maybe later I will tear out these pages.

November 27

I picked today to do the inevitable. I don't know what I was thinking.

I pulled him into the bedroom, shut the door. We have so little time left, I said. I thought you should know.

Before I had even finished the last word, such alarm in his eyes. I don't know what he thought I was going to say and now, in retrospect, I think: He must have thought I was going to confess that I was pregnant or dying or something. Not that there's much difference now whether you say <u>I am with child</u> or <u>I am with sickness</u>. Something like that, but he was pre-emptively startled, worried.

Listen, I said. Since this all began, no one's loved us. Not the way we needed to be loved. And even in the old days, were you ever loved enough? Once upon a time, our parents did; when they were gone, our brothers and sisters and friends gave us support. But did you ever trust them? Fully? No. The full weight could not be put on anyone, it was thought that no one could bear it. Because everything inside us was too heavy. Even before this happened. So maybe you will say that this too is not love, but the mutual acceptance of that weight, each to someone strong enough to carry it. Still, let me call it that. Let me say I love you. I love you.

Once spoken, I wanted to bolt from the room; I thought, Now I must slink away and die of embarrassment. I think I even backed towards the door, ready to murmur apologies. I thought: I will tell him I'm drunk, tell him I'm sick. Tell him I got a brain parasite from forgetting to boil the river water. Tell him the Them got to me.

But I didn't run. I watched his face crumble instead. Sobered, hurt, he sat on the edge of the table and his curls of many colours caught the candlelight so that he appeared momentarily to be wearing a medieval helmet. He had, I thought, more protection than me.

Oh Eva, he said. No.

Even knowing he would say it, I was destroyed. There was no sweetness in hearing my name in his mouth. I thought of the bomb spinning in the dirt the day we met, which blew up half an hour later. That distant percussion, and dust shaking from the leaves of the trees. I sat down too, on the bed, and let everything wash over me in waves of hot and cold. Even knowing, even knowing.

He said, It's a different world now. I can't even look at you and ask myself how I feel.

What, I said carefully, would a reasonable man feel?

He said, You ask me what is reasonable, what I might feel if I were... the truth is, which you know as well as I do, that we cannot answer this any more, that we have not been able to answer this for two years, and that there are no reasonable men left anyway.

Oh, I said. My ears were ringing.

He said, I will tell you what I think is <u>possible</u> to do. But it's not related to reason. It never will be again.

I said, Feelings aren't. Usually. Are they.

He said, I'm still coming with you.

I said, That's good.

He added, And if it comes to it, I will stay behind in the city to let you escape with them across the lake.

No, I said instantly. I couldn't... no. You'd have to come with us. We'd never...

But he was staring at me, in the candlelight, his sharply delineated features as certain as I've ever seen them. Studying my face to see if I would waver.

I said, Fine. If you stay to fight, so will I. The others can run across the lake.

He said, Good.

I said, But only if it comes to it.

Yes. Only if it does.

Later

Oh, for God's sake. It's like a bloody soap opera in here. I am still not too tired to laugh, but I am very nearly too tired to write.

K. found me just after midnight, and he was better about it than I was. Quiet, thoughtful. He said, I would like to beg you, one last time, to reconsider this. It's an unnecessary provocation to Them.

I said, It's only unnecessary if you think that Them keeping the children locked up in a subterranean dungeon is necessary, Konstantin.

He said, Listen. They're safe there. From the statues, the... the other things. They're being guarded. Even fed. They're protected. What kind of world is it out here, in comparison? It's... it's the jungle, it's anarchy, there are still people out there who would snatch them right out of your arms and roast them alive. And you want to drag them across a frozen lake to questionable safety kilometers away.

Don't exaggerate, I said.

He said, You know, it might be temporary. Keeping them there. Maybe just to protect them while Their reign is solidified. And your plan, it's... it's absolutely reckless, it's so dangerous. I've been saying that since the start.

I said, Yes, you have; and I've been saying fuck you.

All the wattage came on in his blue eyes, and behind them was no longer a candleflame but a searchlight. I stared into them, seeing if they had that strange, reflective layer now, like the agents we had seen, but I couldn't tell. Just blue, and the flickering flame. Some people carry the physical badge, that is toothed and notched and cuts the hands. Some people carry something else.

He approached me slowly, held his hands out, took mine. I shouldn't have let him; I should have pulled them away, shown him exactly what I thought of him. His intact hands were warm. Mine were cold and wet.

He said, Then let the others go. Stay here. With me. I'm only asking because I care about you. Because I... over the last few months, I realize I've come to love you. In another world, another time, we'd be together. I...

I said nothing. I think I even felt nothing, not even the little leap of joy or hope I'd feel when someone says the word now. I was so tired. You cannot say 'love' any more, you just cannot. I wanted to say: Oh, you'd say anything. I know which side you're on now.

But I was thinking instead: He knows everything about the plan. If I take my eyes off him he'll be off to his bosses, those great shimmering walls of evil that have come to infest our planet, and They will say: Well done my good and faithful servant, or whatever it is They say.

Look at him, he's not even looking at me. He's looking right through my head to the wall.

I said, I'll think about it, and I let him raise my hands to his lips. His mouth, too, was warm.

When he left I wanted to run around like a headless chicken. We've been betrayed, or we're about to be, or are we? We don't have time. Call off the plan! No, move it up! Forget the ice. We'll figure something out. A backup train. A rowboat. A wagon. Our people throw nothing away, once we get to the outskirts, near the wall, I'm sure we'll...

...I had to physically sit down and sit on my hands for a while, which wasn't a bad thing. They eventually warmed up beneath my thighs. I had to remind myself to breathe. Breathe, dammit! And V. asleep in the other room. For God's sake.

I keep thinking: It would have been better if we had fought. Really fought. If I could have clocked him even once, if I could have justified him going to Them, and saying: She will betray you, look what she did to my face. But instead we are in this uneasy limbo, which I hate more, and the sky screams and chimes, and we are running out of time.

But it is much faster to betray than to build. O, that a man can smile, and smile, and smile, and still be a villain!

November 29

The ice must be almost ready. After breakfast, when the sun is fully up, V. and I will go down and check.

K. is done for me, he's done. I said, directly, quietly, Are you going to turn us in?

And he looked back at me, and then looked away, and he said: No.

That was all I needed to hear, as damning as if he had taken out a badge and thrown it onto the floor between us. I didn't even say: So I was right. I didn't say: I saved your life, you bastard.

I thought, exhaustedly: Did I? Or was it all a play, a sham? Did I fall for it because of something so broken and hungry inside me that I cannot even give it a name?

Still I refuse to give it a name. Still I refuse to say to anyone: Forgive me. I was jealous, I wasn't paying attention. I missed things, so many things, and I let so many things slide past me that I should have caught. I let myself be distracted.

And K. did not. God, I am almost jealous of that too. What a world.

I said, my voice wavering, Can you at least tell me what They want to accomplish here?

He sagged. We both knew exactly what kind of conversation we were having. He said, slowly, They don't tell us, you know. Not in words, not really. It's more like... the nightmares that everyone has. When They are done with one world, They find another, and if there is a way They can avoid doing Their own work on the ground, They use the existing life forms. Here, that's us. Their learning curve seems... clumsy. They carry a time with Them that isn't the same as ours. But...

I said, But you'll be spared.

He said, Yes. And you too, if you...

No, I said. Why wouldn't you turn us in? Tell Them everything? Won't They punish you after this?

He said, I don't know. Yes, probably.

They already know that we're up to something, I said.

Yes.

So you don't need to turn us in at all. It's already been done.

Yes.

I turned away from him; I thought: Don't let yourself be distracted. It's almost done. None of this will matter in... what, a day and a half, two days? None of this will matter. Especially why we did what we did.

He said, You and him...

Him who?

Valentin.

I said, What about him?

And he looked at me with the flame of his eyes flickering behind the blue, turning it into glass, and I thought, I was a fool, I really was, in five or six different ways, to not see this coming, and he said, Nothing. Never mind.

Every family, they say, gets one saint. I wonder who ours is.

November 30

I wish I could so much as... picture a future that includes V. and me, together, alive. We don't end up together. We can't and we don't. Even if, one day, it was love, we could never split our love and loyalty like that. We would never be able to forget these days and the things that were said. Perhaps for other people in the long, long history of war and love, it has happened that way, but not now. And no one else can know.

I fear the things I don't know, not the things I do. I'm afraid of so much and I've never been responsible for so much. I'm so afraid. I'm worried I'll freeze at the moment I can least afford it, and no one will be able to help me. But I am determined to stay and fight, if anyone needs to.

The enemy is not each other and the enemy is not love. It's not wanting to be loved, either. It's so important, I wish I hadn't figured it out so late, but there's no one I can tell any more. Only this paper, only this book, almost full, and so wrinkled and battered: that's not the enemy. That's the ally. The only one we've got. It will not help us win the day. Nothing will. But it will fight at our side.

It will not save us. It will only save our humanity. In the end.

There's coal for the train. A. and I found a big bag of it this morning, and spent forever patiently packing it into paper bags so we can all carry some.

Fireworks last night. Just as we were promised, all those weeks ago.

IN THE HOVER, I watch the landscape pass below us, scarred and cratered, brightly submerged in fields of sunflowers, fluorescent yellow oilseeds, overgrown meadows that need a good graze. Where was that town, I wonder. I don't know which way is west.

No one speaks. I never got my showdown and now it's too late. Life isn't like that, history isn't like that.

There isn't always the big fight that clears the air. The corrupt general doesn't always get overthrown by his men; the evil empress isn't always killed by her slaves; the armistice, so close, doesn't always get signed.

I lean my head back on my seat and think of V., who I liked, and who I thought loved Eva back, and how wrong I was, and now I'm angry at him, and he's probably been dead for decades; and I think of K., who would have looked after her, but who she never would have trusted, just as I never trusted him. And I wanted to. And I don't know why.

My phone pings. I look down tiredly to see that I've gotten an email back from Dr. Aaron: *Thank you for scans of journal. V. interesting. Already asking for funding to return in the spring, investigate tunnel/train, traces around city of successful escape. Unique in SB history. All my best.*

Even this, of course, is not a triumph; I write back asking if we can also assemble the ethics committee, for a private discussion rather than a hearing, about the events that occurred on this research trip, and hit send. And that is not a triumph either. It feels cheap and cold, and does nothing for my anger, or my frustration.

"Why'd you do it?" I say quietly to Darian, who's been strapped in across from me; the others are asleep, or pretending to be.

"Do what?" he says.

"Sabotage my research."

"That is a pretty serious accusation," he says. "Pretty strong wording. I hope you have something just as strong to back that up."

"Just tell me why."

"I don't know what you're talking about." He pauses, and leans close, speaking rapidly, the closest he will come to an admission of guilt. "What's the point anyway? We'll never know what They were! We'll never know where They came from! We can't prevent Them from coming again! All we can do now is use what happened for the future. That's what *I'm* doing. Getting data to build better buildings, stronger foundations. Bunkers for war, to protect soldiers. Even better bombs. And what are you doing? Wallowing in the past with them, and bringing nothing into the future. What's that worth? You were a waste of money on this trip, Emerson. I'm sorry to say it, but your whole project was a waste of money, and the university should know it. Nothing of any worth came out of it. Just historical curiosities."

"They—" I begin, and almost choke on my tears of rage. His look of sympathy is infuriating; how dare he wish to comfort me, when he's the reason I'm so angry. "They fought off the Invaders, they're the reason we're alive today, and not only alive but able to live in comfort, go to school, do research; they're the reason the Setback ever ended. And anyway, you think there *has* to be an application for things we study? You think *everything* has to end up in some... lab somewhere, a product for people to buy? Well, I happen to think there are other questions in the world. Don't you believe in truth? History? Isn't that worth studying and saving? We are the descendants of these survivors, of people who survived in cities that everyone else thought were completely dead. Isn't *that* worth something?"

He shrugs; I flop back in my seat and glare at him.

"You're asking these questions like they're necessary," he says a minute later. "But they don't need to be answered. You would have gotten enough answers just from seeing the city. Didn't you read the last entry?"

"No."

"You should. You should see how it ends."

"Don't tell me what to do. And don't talk to me," I tell him, "till we land."

"All right."

"I mean it."

"All right."

December 1

It is the day.

We cannot wait any longer. Snow lightly falling. Please let it not get any deeper. Our best chance today. I must leave this book. I dare take nothing with me that has no use.

Everything will be taken from us, but only us. They will go on without us, as the world goes on without us.

This was deserved. This was all deserved. Somehow, we did something to deserve this.

This morning, at long last, unneeded, uncalled-for, I remembered the last lines of the damn poem. All I can write before we leave.

Shine out, my sudden angel,
Break fear with breast and brow,
I take you now and for always,
For always is always now.

ACKNOWLEDGEMENTS

I WOULD LIKE to thank my agent, Michael Curry, and my editor, David T. Moore, for believing in this story and giving it a second chance after a rocky and unpromising start.

*And now read a sample of
Premee Mohamed's upcoming novel*

A BROKEN DARKNESS

Coming
2nd March 2021 (US)
4th March 2021 (UK)

978-1-78108-875-3

IF ANYONE KNEW what I knew, they'd say, and rightly so, *You knew everything. She told you everything, at the last. And you took this knowledge purchased literally with your life and you did nothing. It's not too late though. Call the cops. Call the FBI. Call a priest. Arrest her! Do something! But you didn't talk. And she didn't talk.*

We didn't talk. But we'd have to talk tonight, for as I laboured up the slope towards the entrance of the castle, everything made certain to remind me, in case I managed to forget for one second, that this was her party, it belonged to her, she'd paid for it, was the guest of honour, the hero of the hour, and the world's first official Chambers Reactor powered the lights and music.

A lightshow rotated on the damp stone of the castle walls: flags of Scotland and the European Union and the City of Edinburgh, and a tangle of crests, tartans, logos, brands, mascots. Spinning unicorns corkscrewed into a half-dozen Chambers Industries graphics: Chambers

Labs. Chambers Energy. Chambers Biomedical. I imagined a half-dozen interns jealously duelling it out at the projector deck like rival DJs fighting at a rave, elbowing each other aside to get their particular division on the program.

Which was hilarious, because tonight I was pretending to be an intern too: for BGI, the big tech conglomerate. I'd been assigned the internship as a cover (as well as a branded t-shirt, mug, baseball cap, cell phone, and five hundred business cards that I never handed out). Only Society members were supposed to know if you were in the Society or not.

BGI was a good choice. Their employee base worldwide numbered in the faceless and anonymous millions, and they were recognizable enough to be 'prestigious' to Mom and, grudgingly, in our infrequent phone calls, Dad too. They had a vague idea what my job description meant ("Quality assurance and quality control") and were merely proud that I had gotten such a well-paying job in the gap between high school and, she assumed, university.

I hoped I could lie fluently about being in Edinburgh on a work conference, sent as a last-minute replacement for my boss (which was more or less true). Meanwhile, I'd told Mom and the kids I was in Orlando for a different conference (user interface design? something like that). The Society had even figured out how to get my name on the web page; I knew Carla would peek right away. She tried to resist, I knew, but was always cross-checking my movements to see if I was lying to them again. I felt terrible about her compulsion, but I could never tell her the truth; who knew *what* they'd do if I did.

Really though, in my (rented) tux, I was pretending to be James Bond. Like Jude Law in the last couple movies, sleek and arrogant and able to brazen his way through anything. Hadn't mentioned that on the phone to my boss, of course. There hadn't even been a space to apologize for what I'd done to the watcher, nowhere to fit words in through the Niagara-like, billion-ton waterfall of his anger. Only when he had paused to catch his breath did I mention that his daughter, whom I'd thought was studying in Spain, was now in... Edinburgh? Coincidentally, at the Chambers Reactor ribbon-cutting ceremony, to which tickets had been assigned months in advance? What a lucky young lady she was...

Lucky, Louis had said, drawing the word out, and hung up on me.

As I had stood in the kitchen, staring blankly at my phone and trying to think of how to communicate my last wishes to my sleeping family without actually telling them why I might be doing such a thing, he had called back.

Louis's assistant had been quietly calling around; both Sofia's residence manager and her dorm-mate said she had dropped out. Sofia hadn't been seen in weeks, despite the fact that at every call with her father, she had chatted chirpily about her classes and exams.

And one thing had led to another, and here I was, the instigator of this tangle of boss, daughter, nemesis and myself, struggling in the middle of their web like a very confused, though dapper, fly.

From Louis, I had understood, clearly and a little insultingly, that my commitment to the Society was not *distrusted* exactly, but (and I would admit this) undeniably strained: both from the conditions of their discovering me in the first place, and the incident with the watcher. *Do you know what used to happen to people who did what you did? In the old days? Mm?*

Fuck you, I should have said. You're not paying me enough to threaten me.

But I hadn't, and had sat there instead, frightened and fuming, absorbing the familiar refrain: Just pay your dues. Serve your time. I could be so much more than a mere Monitor. I could rise in the ranks. Other people had. I could be prestigious, respected, like the others.

Remembering the kids beaming through their envy, demanding souvenirs from the Kennedy Space Center and Disneyworld. Mom ruffling my hair, running her thumb over my ear. *I'm so proud of you, baby. That's a good sign, when they start giving you more responsibilities.*

Liar, liar, liar, liar. And I'd come back without a tan, too. Just tell them you were listening to talks the whole time, Louis' assistant had said. A strong implication of: Do I have to think of everything? Can you not lie on your own? A Chambers Labs subsidiary was presenting at the conference in Orlando, I had noticed: Lazuli Software Solutions.

Johnny was everywhere, she was like mold spores in the air, nowhere was free of her. You couldn't take one breath without drawing her in, having her grow inside you. Making you sick.

A nasty realization had built while I writhed unsleeping on the plane, and it worsened now, as I joined the line of people waiting to get in, shivering in the cool fog. If it really had been Sofia, her dodging the camera suggested she didn't want to be spotted there. Yet she must have known the ceremony would be filmed—not only that, but broadcast worldwide. Millions, even billions of people must have seen that footage. And she knew that, she would have known that. So why had she gone? What was she up to? And why hadn't she told her dad?

I hadn't seen her in person for months, not since my last training trip to Chicago; she'd been distant, even cool, yet somehow had contrived to run into me, with or without her dad, about a dozen times a day. Afterwards, she kept messaging me on ICQ, a half-hour of cautious small talk each time. We were, I thought, in that uneasy space between strangers and friends, but since I'd never really had friends except Johnny (ow—that stab of hate again), I couldn't tell.

The beams of the lightshow stabbed up through the fog like knives, a guard of honour as I approached the front of the line. Like photos of royal weddings, walking under the bridge of blades. Good thing Louis's assistant had called to get me a tux: under laughably heavy coats, many trimmed with fur or velvet, most people were in tuxedoes too, or else floor-length dresses in a dark rainbow of hues. I hoped no one would look at my boots.

The lady taking names with her laptop stared up at me far too long. I met her eye, daring her to say something, tell me I didn't belong there. Go on. You'll see. The Society is full of these little tricks.

"Nicholas Prasad," I repeated, leaning down. After she looked at my driver's license, she gave me a paper wristband and waved me through. I swiped my sleeve over my face, barely dislodging the clammy mix of perspiration and precipitation.

God, why had I agreed to this bullshit? Some vague impulse fueled by who-knew-what, something I hadn't been able to resist, giving the impression that it was not large but fast-moving, too quick to dodge, about how a man's got to do what a man's got to do, but was this, in fact, *it*?

If it was, I decided, what a man had to do was *incredibly* bad planning.

All the same, what was the worst that could happen? Two girls might be mad at me, and I could call Louis back and confirm that his darling only child was fine. And then home on Monday, with Society-provided memorabilia, mouse ears and rocketships and little bits of gator-shaped tat and glitz. Job safe. Everything fine, and the boat that I had set rocking with my mistake (not to mention ratting out Sofia) would be settled again, safe again.

I walked under a stone arch into a cross-road, thick uneven walls against a clouded sky, feather-soft and without a single star. People milled, murmured, smoked, laughed. There was a strong smell of money; you got it at Johnny's place sometimes, and always at her mother's house. Cigars, cryo-treatments, Botox, lip fillers, hair transplants, expensive perfumes and colognes, aromatherapy orthotics, drycleaning chemicals, real leather, jewels kept in storage. I didn't have that. Would they sniff me out, turn on me? Rented tux, hotel soap. Smell of jetlag. My watch still on Edmonton time.

Metal signposts pointed to *PRISONS OF WAR* and *WAY OUT*, mostly obscured now by large laminated sheets that said *CHAMBERS REACTOR GALA FEBRUARY 6 2004* with a big reflective arrow.

I liked the tall blocky towers, their windows crisscrossed with lead. The stones were all different colours, like camo-print. It wouldn't help if you were being invaded, I thought, but maybe the visual effect would screw up the aim of folks with projectile weapons. How old was this place, anyway? Its age pressed down like the weight of a thunderstorm. *I have everything you don't*, it seemed to say: *mass, history, dignity, culture*. And by 'you' I thought it meant both me and where I was from. No castles back home. Rightly so, I wanted to explain: the land was swindled or taken at gunpoint from people who neither built nor needed them.

Need has nothing to do with it, I pictured the castle replying, *I will be here for thousands of years more, needed or no*.

Conversely, I didn't like the arches, which seemed too heavy to stay up, itching to fall on some tourist. Indoors was a relief despite the stifling heat. Unofficially, I knew, the party filled the entire grounds, and I had seen a few forlorn-looking string quartets and appetizer stations outside in the fog, but in practice, it was cold and grim enough that everyone had crowded into the Great Hall.

The room was half-painted in deep red, half panelled with wood; the stained-glass windows had been strung with small white party lights, bringing their colours to life. Polished armour and dozens of weapons hung on the walls, baroque blades and spikes arranged like fireworks. That was good, actually, very handy. When either Sofia or Johnny started asking the hard questions,

I could just run myself through. Die of blood loss before dying of embarrassment. True, the Society would lose its deposit on the tux, but...

Before I really realized what I was looking at, my body jolted minutely, like the electrical shock of a dry winter day. The hall was lined with nooks like restaurant booths, which I figured were off-limits during tourist hours but were now open; and one of these was occupied by Johnny, lit all gold and dark like an old painting under several skinny standing lights. She was being simultaneously photographed and filmed by two people, and interviewed by three others, pivoting back and forth at their conflicting cues and the demands of the lenses.

I parked myself behind a big guy in a white jacket who was offering trays of what Johnny called 'tiny bits of junk on sticks' (her nemesis; she always ate before parties). The crowd eddied like one of those fancy aquariums in the mall, deep water of tuxedoes, bright coral of gowns, jewelry like darting fish. Hm. Save up, get a suit like that back home: silky blue or green or violet under the lights, black in the shadows. Couple of iridescent ties. Start going to clubs.

Some people stared despite my tux, but after I snagged a glass of champagne, I abruptly achieved invisibility; their gazes hit and slid off. I held my nose over the cold skinny glass, enjoying the tickle of the popping bubbles.

The lighting left the musicians (six of them—what was that? a hexet? a sextet?) and the high ceiling in darkness. In the center of the room, someone had poised a spotlight on something I couldn't see through the crowd, glassy-looking, maybe an ice sculpture. Like that one Nobel-watching party we'd gone to at the university, where we had gotten kicked out after she—

That sting again. Stop it, stop remembering her as human. It was all lies, goddammit. You know that. Stick to your job.

I scanned the room for Sofia and gingerly let my champagne soak into the apparently parched scrubland of my tongue; it had no taste at all, only texture, as if I had drunk a mouthful of tacks. Two mouthfuls later I was thirstier than before. I glared at it.

"Want some smoked salmon?"

The fourth sip exited my mouth in a fine mist; Johnny dodged it absentmindedly, and held up her plate.

"Come off it," she said. "Like it's so shocking to see *me* here, with my name all over the signs. What are *you* doing here? How did you get in? I didn't put your name on the list."

"Don't just sneak up on people like that!"

"Uh-huh. Should I call security or what?"

I glanced around in automatic alarm. The security I had expected, her assistant Rutger, who first of all didn't like me, and secondly was about twice as big as me on every axis, was nowhere to be seen. The two dark-suited people behind her were unfamiliar—stiffly alert, watching me with Rutger-caliber disdain.

She followed my gaze. "He's back at the hotel. Wanted to review some data. You know Elizabeth and Wayne."

I nodded as if I did. While I waited to see which of my various sphincters had either fused shut from shock or were on the verge of letting go, she complacently made a tiny burrito out of a pancake, some smoked salmon, a scoop of caviar, and pickled onion. "Here. Eat this."

"Where did you get this?"

"Buffet at the back," she said, expertly wrapping up another one. "Asked the caterers for it. Can't stand that little-shit-on-sticks situation."

I glared downwards. Her boyish, Gap-commercial haircut had been recently touched up; the ends seemed fresher, brassier, like fine wire. If she'd done her own makeup, she'd done a piss-poor job of it; the gold glitter on her eyes had escaped into her eyebrows and even her nose and chin. Under a weirdly short but long-sleeved sweater, her knee-length black dress was belted with a chain of Oreo-sized golden discs. It made me think of ancient Greece: a famous vase, maybe, or a picture in one of the kids' books.

Her eyes, steadily meeting mine, were the same as ever: that sinister green, the green of a Disney villain's eyes, if anything more yellow than I remembered. Sickly, even inhuman. Like an animal. I reached inside myself, felt for the old love, the new hate, and felt only revulsion, the instinctive recoiling from a monstrous stranger who had stolen a beloved face, a familiar voice, and now wore them proudly, showing them off to the horrified survivors.

"Okay, listen," I said.

"Listening." She took my champagne glass and drained it, then handed it to a passing server without looking.

Something warm slid through my arm and grasped my wrist, and this time I yelped out loud and jerked backwards into the wood panelling. The thing clung like a tentacle, but in the split second before I drew my fist back (good God: to do *what*, exactly?) I realized what was happening and tried to recover, picturing how it must have looked—the squawk, the sluggish flinch and twitch, the noise (had I imagined it?) as my head hit the wood. I hoped no one had been filming us.

Face hot, double-0 status revoked, I crooked my elbow where Sofia had taken it, and managed something that I hoped looked like a smile. She was a shimmering presence at my side, like a mirror, or those polished refractor things the ancient Greeks or whoever aimed at ships during wars to burn them up; I couldn't look directly at her.

"Sofia!" Johnny said. "What a nice surprise! And holy shit, your earrings. And your *dress!*"

"Thank you! I just bought it this afternoon, especially for tonight!"

"Glgk," I said.

Sofia went on, smoothly, "And thank you for being flexible about the guest list! Security is so important these days."

"Yeah, can't be too careful. Any sort of riff-raff might just wander in."

To her credit, Sofia didn't even glance at me. "I agree, you do not want questionable people at something like this."

As they chatted, I slowly put it together: two Society members were supposed to have been here tonight, but couldn't make it (I wondered if Sofia had pushed them into the ocean). Sofia had been sent unexpectedly at the last moment instead, but Louis had been unable to make it.

"Everyone was very insistent that the Society be represented tonight. It's an historic event! And you were kind enough to ensure we got in. And of course," she added, squeezing my arm, "I hope you do not mind that I used the other ticket for my love here, even though he is not with us! I was hoping we could get some photos while we are all dressed up."

"Of course I don't mind. Two surprises for the price of one. Oh, you should go pose with the armour!" Johnny pointed back at the alcove she'd been in. "The light is still set up, the photographers are paid all night, and you get the painting too. You'll just have to wait for... who is that, is that the Princess of Monaco?"

"No, that's her sister."

"Doesn't that make her a princess too?"

"Not after what happened last week."

I wondered if this was death, if my soul was even now leaving my body, floating up into the ceiling, passing through it sadly into the sky (or, let's be realistic, down into the Earth's core to be incinerated). How was I supposed to figure out what Sofia was doing now? Louis wouldn't care that I'd been set up somehow, or by who. He'd just kill me. If you could kill someone who was already dead, which...

Sofia surreptitiously pinched my wrist, producing a bolt of pain from my fingertips to my ear. "Sounds good," I croaked.

"Well, you both look like a million bucks," Johnny said, reaching out surreptitiously to tug up one side of my cummerbund. "You should *totally* get some nice pictures. Especially you, Nick; you're always on the wrong side of the camera, you got all those photos of the kids and none of you. Your mom deserves at least one nice shot up there somewhere. Like, *one*."

"Mmpt."

"And maybe Sofia has a comb you can use?"

"Eckff."

"I'll see what can be done," Sofia chuckled.

Belatedly—possibly because, as far as I could tell, I was dead—Sofia's absolute conniving cleverness dawned on me. How else would you explain me being there? Her, you could explain. She wasn't a Society member, but she was a representative all the same; in fact, Louis had always tried to keep her as far from their business as possible. She was just the eternal and permissible coworker's kid, allowed at their events and parties since she had been little, the way the dealers and bartenders had fondly looked away when Mom used to bring me to her shifts at the casino.

I realized that I had been expecting, for at least a couple of minutes, to see something resembling irritation or jealousy on Johnny's face, and then was annoyed at myself, and then was annoyed that I was annoyed. I tried to freeze my face into an expression of pleasant unsurprise.

Sofia announced, "Let's go see if the photographer is free!"

But a moment after we wandered away, the smile dropped off her face with an audible thud. "What are you doing here, Nicholas?"

"Uh, having a panic attack."

"Oh, God," she groaned. "You can always trust boys to have the stupidest answer out of a choice of millions... I recommend you *try again*. And *fast*."

"Are you about done? Jesus. Your dad sent me. Obviously."

"What? Why?"

I blinked. Had I not said *obviously*? I was sure I had. "Because he was worried about you. Because he called campus, and they said you dropped out. Why do you *think*?"

"I assumed you were here for *her*. Why wouldn't you be?"

"Lots of reasons," I said.

"My father has no need to send... nannies after me. I'm not a child."

"Nobody said you were! Calm down. He's worried, he says you were lying to him. About being in school. The school said you dropped out. He was going to come find you himself, but he couldn't make it. What are you trying to pull, anyway? They're not gonna do anything to you, but who even *knows* what they'll do to me?"

She blinked, having clearly stopped listening to me halfway through my rant. The anger drained away from her face, leaving a terrible uncertainty and betrayal, the expression of a kid promised something only to have it suddenly yanked away. A moment later it was gone, and she was all business again.

Somehow, even in formalwear, she looked businessy too: the long, silvery-blue dress was cut like a suit at the top, and she was wearing heels so high we were eye to eye. Makeup too, dark lipstick and eyeshadow, metallic on her deep brown skin. Her long hair was tied back, the curls in front ferociously bobbypinned; the crisscrossed metal resembled a secret language. A cuneiform curse, no doubt.

But her face. Don't lose track of that. Saying into the silence: *He sent you? After all I did to rig it so that he would be here tonight?*

I said, "He said he was going to send his new... what do you call it. Secretary?"

"Assistant."

"Yeah, Sherwood or whoever. Is that his first name or his last name? Anyway, Louis thinks he's too new. So he sent me. So it would be less weird."

It's still weird, her sneer said. "Let's look over here instead!" she announced, pulling me further towards the perimeter of the room, then hissed, "I'm on spring break. I'm allowed to go on holiday, you know!"

I shook my arm free. "Look, are you going to tell me what you're doing or not?"

"Nothing! This is unbelievable. He sent you all this way, and you—you said yes, you agreed to come all this way! To what, spy on me? It's *nothing*, I got a cheap flight, and I had plans with friends, they did not work out this week, then I decided I would still come by myself."

"Okay," I said. "You know. For the weather. Which is so nice. In Scotland. In February."

"People don't travel for the *weather*, Nicholas."

Johnny was wandering back towards us, the blonde head bumping through the crowd. Like the shark from *Jaws,* but little. I held down a laugh that I knew would come out in a donkey screech.

"Now knock it off or I'll tell her everything," Sofia whispered, and smiled again, brilliantly, as she took my hand.

"Me? You're the one who—"

"Yeah, and on *top* of the bull," Johnny was saying even before she reached us, "we're actually being audited by the IARE too. It started off as just a health and safety thing, but they've got the entire ethics department involved now. They think multiple facilities are falsifying and publishing data. Can you believe it?"

"Incredible!" Sofia shook her head.

I pursed my lips. She'd been audited before, though mostly for safety stuff; it was both horrifying and unsurprising how many accidents she'd had, apparently thinking that safety standards were something for other people. They hadn't found anything at her facilities, as a result, but at a *minimum* I knew she'd been burned by acid, had a few solvent inhalation incidents, got blasted with one of her early particle accelerators (luckily at low power), been on the sharp end of ten or twelve explosions—I'd lost count—poisoned herself, fallen off ladders, cabling, catwalks, rigging, and bookshelves in her ridiculous house-slash-laboratory, been electrocuted about six times, and Chem-Bot had accidentally sampled part of her arm once. And that entirely left out the dozens of incidents where genetically-screwed-up insects and plants had escaped 'containment'—usually a carelessly-lidded plastic tub, as I'd discovered more than once while scavenging for a snack.

She ran her empire in roughly the same fashion as ancient kings insisting on going to war personally rather than staying in the castle and moving pieces on the map with a wooden stick. But that was something. The audit... why would the Society be here for that?

"There's a completely private one for my personal

guests," Johnny was saying when I tuned back in. My watcher-wounded hand had started to hurt for some reason, quietly building, as if ice were forming from some tiny core within it. "Down that hallway, and you'll see a guy in a dark green suit? Tell him I sent you, and say 'Independent review.'"

"What?"

"You'll see," she laughed.

Sofia disentangled herself, gave me a peck, and slipped through the crowd, her dress a trickle of mercury through all the dark fabrics. Where her lips had touched my cheek felt like a cigarette burn.

"Let's go get some more food." Johnny wriggled out of her sweater and handed it to Wayne, who folded it neatly to the size of a paperback book and placed it inside his own jacket pocket.

The crowd parted almost frantically around us. Her touch phobia, which to this day I wasn't sure was real or staged, was well-known, in fact had literally been the subject of a documentary once, and although many palms hovered in congratulations over her bared shoulders, people probably knew they would have set off, at best, a crying jag and a swift retreat, or, at worst (and it had so often been worst) a couple of swift blows ending in broken collarbones, fingers, or jaws. Even a dislocated shoulder once, I remembered. An older man had touched her from behind and... bad angle. Bad land. She struck out like a bee, not strategizing, just looking to jam in her sting and flee. It had disappeared after the Anomaly, or her stubborn maintenance of the act had slackened off, but no one else here could know that.

Near the fireplace, the room was stifling; sweat gathered in my hairline and crawled down my face. I heaped up plates of random food in the low scarlet light, handed one to Johnny, and, although I was beginning to suspect she was already a little drunk, let her get two more glasses of champagne. Or no, what was the word…?

"Flutes, Nicky," she said airily, as if I had projected it from my head like the lightshow outside. "Chug, chug. It won't go flat right away but it's kinda gross when it gets warm."

Her tone was affectionate, familiar. If I hadn't spent so long remembering and recreating everything she had done to me, it would have been so easy to just… tell her everything. Fall back into the deep permanent me-shaped rut that she *wanted* me to see was still there, and still perfectly intact, even though we were both so different now. *Look*, she was saying. *I won't treat you any differently. Everything you miss is waiting for you. Everything you've been missing during this long, cold self-enforced solitary sentence. See, I don't even mind your girlfriend, or you not telling me. Because we're best friends. Blood brothers. Aren't we?*

I took the glass and we wandered away from the fire into relatively cooler air. I'd play along, no more. Couldn't she see, she who had known me all my life, that I wasn't hers anymore? That she had thrown me away by telling me the truth? At the very least, could she not fucking tell that I had a higher mission now than being her *pet*?

Anyway, I'd put something on her plate that I hadn't put on mine, and I wanted it. "What's that?"

"Stuffed mushroom, I think."

"Stuffed with what?"

"Haggis."

I frowned, and stabbed it with my tiny fork. "I thought a haggis was a whole... thing. Like I'm picturing an animal the size of a volleyball."

"I think that's a weirdly common misconception."

I drained my flute, the bubbles crackling between my teeth. The second glass of champagne, I decided, was better than the first. More like fine-grit than coarse-grit sandpaper. But it still left me desperately thirsty. "What's *in* this stuff?"

"I know, it does the same thing to me. I think it's a rich people conspiracy to sell more champagne."

"You're a rich people."

"No, I just have money. *They're* rich." Her apparently casual gesture at the crowd somehow managed to hand off her empty glass and swap it with a full one; she gave it to me. I wiped my face with my sleeve again. My left hand hurt so badly it was taking an increasing amount of concentration not to clench it into a fist, and break the delicate glass.

"So," she said. "You and Sofia."

"Uh."

"Is that what you were going to tell me earlier?"

"No."

She smiled, a careful selection from her arsenal, one I knew well: sly, self-satisfied, slow, only wavering for a second when it seemed I wouldn't react to it.

"I thought it was so *romantic*," she breathed, "the way she came in half an hour before you did."

"What? No, she didn't."

From her belt she unclipped a phone case I hadn't noticed, black leather with a glittery unicorn sticker on it. "So, the station up front where you got your wristband? That laptop is synced up with my records. Neat, huh? And so nice to see that you... managed to reunite after meeting once? It's like something from a movie. Like *Cinderella*. You Prince Charming, you."

You know what? You're one to fucking talk. You were sneaking around behind the scenes for my entire life, making sure anyone who might have loved me or even liked me suddenly had to move away or switch schools, got fired from their jobs or transferred to another country. You think I've forgotten? Or you're forgiven? Looking up at me like that, so innocent?

But we couldn't talk about it. Still. Never.

The room swam with heat and pain as I tried to focus on a real response. Of course Johnny thought we'd only met once. In Fes, when Sofia had appeared out of nowhere, saving both our asses. What was the obvious...? "Okay, not that it's any of your business, but yeah, she did find me afterwards. It wasn't like you made me hard to find. We talk a lot on ICQ and stuff, this is the first time we've seen each other in... listen, the main thing is, we have to keep it on the down-low from her dad. He doesn't want her to date while she's in school. He'd be pissed. *Pissed*, she says."

"Totally hear you," Johnny said. "He used to say it all the time. Even when she was little. You know. *No boys. Keep your eyes on your books. Boys are evil. Only after one thing.*"

"Yeah, you get it."

"Mm. So that must be why she took you to this party," she went on, jerking her chin at the room. "A big, public event, with scientists and celebrities and politicians and royalty. Where you'd be filmed together. And photographed together. And that the Society's had two tickets to since last September. Makes perfect sense."

"None of my business," I said again. "I got nothing to do with those weirdos. I'm here for the free food. And what's that over there?" I said, gesturing at the pedestal in the middle of the room.

"Nice subject change. Come look at my pride and joy," she said. "You may as well, since you came all this way just for... the party. I'll show Sofia when she comes back from the bathroom, too. Not everybody is getting the personal tour, you know."

"Poor them."

It wasn't an ice sculpture as I had thought, but a glass dome over a tiny model of a building, perched atop an island the size of a paperback book. It might have been made out of paper-thin folded metal. "What is this, a reactor for ants?" I said.

"I know, right? The thing is, the working part of the real reactor is about the size of a hockey puck, but you can't just put something that small out there. It needs to look legit. People get nervous if it doesn't."

She tapped the dome with her glass, making everyone around us cringe at the noise. "*This* is my favourite thing. We're not doing a lot of transparent nanoceramic because of the interactive bond-degradation problem, but I begged them to make enough for the model. It took months. I utterly degraded myself. *We're not worthy, we're not worthy!*"

"Yeah. I bet."

"And then I came over and me and Wing ran it over with one of the lab trucks to see if it would break. It was awesome."

"...Ran *this* over?"

"We buffed out the tiremarks afterwards. You could blast this with a railgun and it probably wouldn't break." She paused, thinking, and sipped her champagne. "It might chip. Anyway, generation is fully automated, but there's remote control just in case. See, there's the signal array. We used the experimental molpoxy on it, the entire roof will rip off before that dish does. On the building, I mean, not here. *This* is all held together with superglue. The torus and shielding goes there, under the red X. Except I forgot to put one on the mockup so I had to borrow some nail polish from one of tonight's makeup guys."

"A professional did your makeup? I hope you didn't pay them."

"Shut up. I kept touching my face during the photoshoot. Anyway, I made sure the reactor is about the size of a golf cart, and the rest of the building is mostly safety stuff in case of storms or seismicity, and smart grid control systems to regulate the subaqueous cable distribution load and deal with surges. And make sure that it's tuned to... to avoid... the problem we had when it was initially developed."

"The," I said slowly, "problem."

She tilted her chin defiantly, as if one of us had said,

Are you referring to the 'problem' that accidentally but very nearly ended the world? "I've had trial versions running with no issues, no harmonics. Oh, and down there, that's the pod system for personnel in case the drones can't reach the island."

"And what's that?"

"What's what?"

"That," I said, touching the top of the dome, where a half-dozen small, shiny orbs had been meticulously painted on the underside. "Is it for measurements or whatever? Wind? Waves? Are those weather balloons?"

"Um." She blinked.

As one, our chins dragged themselves to the vertical, pinning our horrified stares on the high, crossed beams of the ceiling where the light refused to go.

"Remember that one time we rode our bikes north of town," she whispered, "and—"

"—went to that old grain elevator because—"

"—I wanted to test my cyclonic densities detector, and it was full of..." She carefully put her glass on the pedestal, without looking down.

"Oh, man," I said, still staring. "It would be *awesome* if those things were bats."

And, as if it had only been waiting for us to meet its gaze, darkness descended.

THE THINGS BILLOWED down in silence, formless and lazy as parachutes, so that for the first moments people smiled up at them, maybe thinking it was some kind of art installation. But Johnny dove to the ground, rolling away from the roped pedestal, and I did too, just as the screaming began: one high, terrified note, quickly joined by dozens of others.

"Everybody outside!" someone cried, but it trailed off into an awful, wet gurgle. Ballgowns and shining shoes flowed past us like water, confused with other bright things: eyes that were not eyes, just membranous lights; hair that wasn't hair but strings of slime; feathers as far from feathers as anything you'd see in a nightmare; and worst of all, recognizably human, or imitating a human: familiar skulls, femurs, eyes mindless with pain. Feet hammered against my shoulders as I rolled into a ball, watching for Johnny, the bright winks of her metal belt.

Many of the creatures were pulsating far outside the normal spectrum, hues you'd only see in sigils. The palms of their hands stuttered and flashed like strobe lights, sending people unseeing into the walls, to be quickly picked up by scavenging beasts while they lay stunned. Others extruded what I took to be streams of bubbling liquid but quickly proved to be tentacles, stabbing through clothing and into spines, wearing people like dangle-legged puppets high in the air, screaming and scrabbling for their pierced backs.

People fell, were swarmed at once, flung into the air, released to fall howling into thrashing nests of teeth and limbs, splattered ichor, humans and human-monsters trading identical blows. The hall echoed with voices, the clang of dislodged weapons, crash of broken wood and bone. Someone pulled the fire alarm and that did it: time slowed to a crawl, and everything glanced off the surface of my eyes instead of sinking in.

Up, one hand crunching over broken crystal: the bloodied rainbows of a highball glass etched with thistles. Where had Johnny gone? Her security people surely—no. Smothered in flapping wings and claws, two gunshots virtually unheard over the noise of the alarm, three shots, four, a spray of them, why would you *stop* shooting once you'd started, why did they have *guns*? Something whined past my nose: not a bullet but a human head, bodiless, mouth filled with tentacles, the tiny wings behind either ear pitted and oozing.

A semaphore of flashing discs: there. Johnny hadn't gone far, only crouched behind the pedestal with a silver hors-d'oeuvre tray. Good idea actually. I picked one up myself and ducked instinctively as something swooped over my head, catching in my hair for a moment with a skittering *skritch* That told me it had hit scalp. I flailed at it, snarling, but it was long gone, lost in the commotion.

What spells did I know to fuck something up in here? I couldn't remember. Maybe they hadn't taught me any. Probably for the best. My brain was flying in a million directions, couldn't even focus to see properly, my vision seemed washed out with fireworks of panic. At least the room was still emptying, the walking-wounded dragging the just-plain-wounded, occasionally picking up a monster that seemed more human than the others, releasing them with a cry of disgust. The escape was jittery, stop-and-start, chaos as people stopped to fight the creatures at the doors, creating bottlenecks. The human puppets swooped down, away, back, mobbing, screaming, scrabbling at people's faces and tossing them aside.

Johnny squealed as someone descended on her, clawing at her bare shoulders. As she kicked it away, I walloped it with the tray, casting around for a weapon—the *walls*, for Chrissake!

I made it about two steps before she grabbed my wrist, and I turned in surprise only to realize that it actually *was* a tentacle this time. Hitting it did nothing; I turned my head away, shouting helplessly as the mass of purplish bulges and glittering teeth began to drag me away from the sword-covered walls. Its face was half-familiar, bearded, all too human except where the eyes had been replaced with something else.

Flailing at the thing with my free arm, I unexpectedly fell on my face as it crashed into something and lost its grip, leaving my wrist with a burnt-looking ring and a dozen spots of bloodied flesh. Broken? Hope not. I spun again while it was distracted and wrenched a sword loose from its display—massive, ancient, blunt, with a chipped metal handle that stuck at once to the oozing cuts on my palm.

Then it came into crystal focus, like a lens had swung down; Johnny met my eye and I heard her think it too, clear as words. Oh, shit. Oh, Christ. It can't be.

The monsters weren't trying to kill her.

They were trying to *capture* her.